T0022484

THE CITY OF UNSPEAKABLE FEAR

THE CITY OF UNSPEAKABLE FEAR

JEAN RAY

TRANSLATED BY SCOTT NICOLAY

WAKEFIELD PRESS

CAMBRIDGE, MASSACHUSETTS

This translation © 2023 Wakefield Press

Wakefield Press, P.O. Box 425645, Cambridge, MA 02142

Originally published as *La cité de l'indicible peur* in 1943. This English edition is published by special arrangement with Alma éditeur, France, in conjunction with their duly appointed agents L'Autre agence and 2 Seas Literary Agency.
© Héritier Jean Ray, 2016 et Alma éditeur, Paris, 2016

Cover image: Clip # 04455, *Dienstfertoger Schutzmann* (original French title unidentified, Pathé Frères, 1913) from the Turconi collection at the George Eastman Museum.

All rights reserved. No part of this book may be reproduced in any form by any electronic or mechanical means (including photocopying, recording, or information storage and retrieval) without permission in writing from the publisher.

This book was set in Garamond Premier Pro and Helvetica Neue Pro by Wakefield Press. Printed and bound by Sheridan Saline, Inc., in the United States of America.

ISBN: 978-1-939663-90-0

Available through D.A.P./Distributed Art Publishers
75 Broad Street, Suite 630
New York, New York 10004
Tel: (212) 627-1999
Fax: (212) 627-9484

10 9 8 7 6 5 4 3 2 1

CONTENTS

TRANSLATOR'S INTRODUCTION

Fish or Foul Play

The 1965 and 1971 paperback editions of *La cité de l'indicible peur* from Bibliothèque Marabout-Fantastique feature spectacular covers that are among the most beautiful to grace any of the French-language editions of Jean Ray's work. The two paintings, both the work of the wonderful Belgian artist Henri Lievens (1920–2000), depict essentially the same scene: a hillside village of Medieval-looking stone buildings gripped by tentacles of eerie green mist that weave through the town's streets and alleys, ensnaring the community in an ominous stranglehold and gathering at their center into a shape that suggests the head of a giant octopus. Although Lievens painted the two images several years apart, the only major difference between them lies in their point of view, which is a three-quarter perspective on the 1965 edition and a frontal view on the version from 1971. The latter, on which the colors are also far more vivid, adds an additional detail: two angular, baleful eyes stare back at the viewer from the "head," suggesting some monstrous cephalopod behind the foggy tendrils.

These illustrations serve rather well for the book's opening, but they are somewhat misleading in regard to most of the novel. That the architecture on both covers bears more than a little resemblance to Ray's hometown of Ghent in Belgium than to anywhere in the UK where the novel is set is not a problem, as Ray tell us early on that his fictional English country town of Ingersham "baffles the uninformed visitor by looking more like a village in Flanders than a town in Middlesex or Surrey." However, no giant spectral cephalopods appear in this story, although they certainly exist elsewhere *chez* Jean Ray. And in fact, precious little mist swirls herein either—surprisingly little, considering the degree to which mist, fog, and all sinister occluding vapors are a staple of Ray's fiction.

Such a bait-and-switch approach was hardly unusual during the great paperback era of the first few decades after the Second World War, when lurid covers promising more than their books could deliver were the norm for the work of everyone from Nobel Prize winners to the most disposable pulp authors; the French editions of *The City of Unspeakable Fear* were not remotely the worst offenders of this kind. As metaphorical interpretations, Lievens's paintings are entirely legitimate. But they offer perhaps false expectations regarding the amount of supernatural activity that the reader will encounter. And if you, the reader, come to this book after having already read some or all of Wakefield Press's previous English editions of Jean Ray's work, including such masterpieces as *Cruise of Shadows* and *Malpertuis*, you might approach *The City of Unspeakable Fear* with expectations of something similar, regardless of whether you have seen the French editions.

The City of Unspeakable Fear has the unfair disadvantage of being the "other novel" of an author whose first novel is rightly considered a masterpiece. It is not, by any means, his *only* other novel, but it is his only other full-length adult novel written in French under the name of Jean Ray: most of Ray's other novels, written under various pseudonyms, are either short, written for young readers, and/or in Dutch (it is worth noting that *Geierstein*, the only full-length adult novel he wrote in Dutch, has received favorable comparisons to *Malpertuis*). *City* is a rather different novel from *Malpertuis* and deserves consideration on its own terms. One should not begin it expecting the same levels of deep weirdness that define its slightly older but more celebrated sibling (the two novels were both released in 1943, just a few months apart, with *Malpertuis* first). If one is going to compare *The City of Unspeakable Fear* to any of Ray's other books, the one to look at is his celebrated debut collection, *Whiskey Tales*. If you have read *Whiskey Tales*, you will find here many of the same elements you may have enjoyed there: the dark humor, the macabre, the Dickensian portraits of the criminal demimonde, and the never-ending cat-and-mouse games of police and thieves (thankfully you will *not* encounter here the moments of antisemitism that provided the only sour notes in that first collection). The progression from *Whiskey Tales* to *The City of Unspeakable Fear* seems entirely natural, and the two books complement each other in many of their best aspects.

This novel is also Ray's great homage to Dickens, Chaucer, Shakespeare—and Arthur Conan Doyle (although he never mentions the latter's name herein). And above all, *The City of Unspeakable Fear* is Ray's valentine to the UK, where he set so much of his work, especially *Whiskey Tales*. These British settings, fictional as they may be, and however much they draw on Ray's Belgian home, inspired some of his loveliest and most lyrical passages. I feel that I have done those lines justice here, and I am confident that if you give yourself over to them, they will transport you to imaginary old Ingersham—right to the middle of the precarious period when that town lay in the grip of the Great Fear.

The aforementioned 1971 paperback edition of *The City of Unspeakable Fear*, with its stunning cover and striking color saturation, also presented a brief question in the form of a subtitle that has not appeared on any other edition. This short text asked the reader to consider whether the novel is "a detective novel or a horror novel" (*roman policier ou roman d'épouvante*). One gets the impression that the editors themselves did not know the answer and decided to throw the decision back to the reader. I suspect that, in so doing, they came quite close to Ray's original intent—so much so that I suggest reading *The City of Unspeakable Fear* with that question in mind. I promise the reader will find this an engaging challenge, even after reaching the end. One will also do well to keep in mind the famous line from *Hamlet* that Ray cites several times herein. You will not find giant cephalopods, werewolves, or the last of the Greek gods here, but you will find a surprisingly complex and intricately crafted novel that combines humor, horror, and ratiocination while defying the boundaries of genre at a time when they were still being established. Is *The City of Unspeakable Fear* a detective novel, a horror novel, or something else entirely, something all its own? That mystery, dear reader, is now yours to investigate.

THE CITY OF UNSPEAKABLE FEAR

Opening: "Them . . ."

"Them . . ."

Can these brief opening pages truly illuminate the night? Do they hold the power to light the mystery hunter's lantern? One dare not say.

Did the "Great Fear" that has lurked behind the scenes of English history for nearly five centuries play a part in the multifaceted tragedy of Ingersham?

.   .   .   .

We are in the second half of the fourteenth century.

Chaucer has completed some of his wonderful *Canterbury Tales*. He has known fame, fortune, honors. However, as a disciple of Wycliff,[1] he fights without profit for the religious reform that is brewing across Europe. Unrest has broken out in England, the Lord Mayor of London stands accused, along with Chaucer, his close associate. The author, secretly warned, flees just as the Regent's guards come to arrest him. He petitions for asylum in Holland, Flanders, Hainaut.[2] But exile weighs on him and he returns secretly to England.

He spends the night in Southwark,[3] a town dear to him.

A strange murmur awakens him and draws him to the window.

He sees a troop of pale and silent men wander through the dark street; they carry torches with ghastly flames and, suddenly, from the very mist and moonlight, they construct threatening walls: a prison!

Chaucer understands that these creatures are not of this world, and that they herald the loss of his freedom.

A heartrending voice hurls an unfamiliar name into the silence of the night: Wat-Tyler![4]

Chaucer did indeed experience a bitter sojourn in the Tower's jail, but he naturally remained ignorant of Wat-Tyler and the terrible rebellion of 1640, the one he helped prepare, three centuries before it broke out.

Much later, having regained his honor, in his sylvan retreat at Woodstock, he will speak in hushed words of the prophetic vision, and will designate the ghost builders of smoke jails with this word full of terror and incomprehension: "*Them . . .*"

. . . .

One hundred years later, as the year 1500 approaches, hordes of starving people, burning with fever, descend from Caledonia, sowing their corpses from Balmoral to Dumfries. They neither steal nor beg . . . they run, fall, and die shouting: *They* are coming! *Them . . .*

The Cheviots highlanders leave their oak log homes and join the fugitives, proclaiming the horrible coming of *Them . . .*

Who are THEY? We will never know, because the harbingers of the Great Fear die without revealing their dreadful secret.

. . . .

1610: The mayor of Carlisle[5] is about to sit down to table; he will serve his finest to some friends and notables of the region.

The trout of Eden roast over a clear fire; turbot from Solway are paired with Spanish wines; the Cumbrian forest has provided ample venison; the first grouses make a succulent contribution to the menu. A famous Bradford roasting chef has traveled leagues and leagues in a horse-drawn carriage to bake pâtés, fine oat cakes, buttered darioles, and French-style nougats.

The autumn evening is sweet as can be; in the streets, a procession with lanterns passes to the song of fifes.

The guests take their seats, pour wines from Portugal and Italy. The procession has disappeared, the songs die off in the distance, the last lanterns vanish into the evening's blue shadow.

Suddenly there is a sinister clamor: "*They* are coming!"

People run, brandishing torches and pitchforks. Someone shouts: "To the gates! To the gates!" The feasts are interrupted, the mayor gives orders to the watch, to the volunteer halberdiers, to the king's armed forces who are stationed in his good city.

They . . . never arrive, the moonlit countryside remains deserted; but the next day three hundred people are found *dead of fear* in the city, and among them are seven of the mayor's guests.

We will never know why.

. . . .

That same year, Anne Boleyn's ghost appeared in the Tower, and one hundred and twelve people were strangled in London by . . . ghosts. Podgers[6] described them, however: they barely had human form, and all one could see, springing from misty and amorphous torsos, were their huge cutthroat hands.

. . . .

1770: Preston[7] is a joyless town; indeed, it remains so to this very day, and nothing suggests it won't continue to be so, but life is good there, and peaceful. The inhabitants have remained faithful to their Puritan sects; they are people of common sense, practical, greedy for gain, and enemies of anything that borders on fantasy.

One day, a Sunday of closed doors and windows, dedicated to prayers, hymns, and Bible readings, the alarm bells begin to clang in the six towers of the pious city.

"*They* are here!"

From the top of the walls, people can be seen fleeing into the countryside; the boatmen of the Ribble hurry toward the city with great strokes of their oars.

Mayor Sedwick Evans sends a troop of armed men to meet the uncertain enemy.

Barely half of that force will return to the walls at nightfall. They met with no one, but they left thirteen men dead in the countryside, and twenty more fled to the sea screaming in terror. They won't return.

What happened? No one knows . . . The Great Fear has come.

.   .   .   .

Does this mysterious fear, this silent assault of the invisible, arise periodically on the great island? One is tempted to believe so.

Monsters continue to appear suddenly from the icy waters of Loch Ness; Jack the Ripper, master of London's terror, remains a possibility. Brownies still dance in the moonlight over the Scottish moors and lead travelers into bottomless ravines and lakes.

The Banshee, death's fey, sings by cursed midnight, and the Tower will be peopled eternally with bloody specters.

Did the Terror, citizen by right of England's towns and villages, take shape in Ingersham, to tug there, with its hideous hands of mist, on the strings of human puppets?

Logic says no, but in the face of the Great Fear, it is nothing but a panicked bird that flies to the horizon with wings spread wide, leaving the men who still find hope in it without protection or defense.

I

Sidney Terence or Sigma Triggs

Sidney Terence Triggs was never a policeman.

His father, Thomas Triggs, who during his lifetime was a gamekeeper on the estates of Sir Broody, destined him, in his fatherly dreams of glory, to the noble career of arms.

In Aldershot[1] they remember Sidney Terence Triggs as a helpful boy, very gentle and subject to bullying like no other, despite his powerful build and considerable physical vigor. He did not rise to any rank there, nor, it seems, did he ever apply for one.

He was one of the Rochester Guards; but Colonel Arrow, a fat donkey pickled in whiskey, disliked him and made his existence painful.

Sir Broody's patronage earned him, at the end of his voluntary service, a place in the Metropolitan Police.

For ten months he directed traffic at the intersection of Old Ford Road, perhaps the quietest in Bow. He made endless blunders, and without him this mellow spot would have seen fewer traffic jams, and drivers and cyclists might have been spared many scratches and bruises.

Sir Broody intervened just as S. T. Triggs's bosses advised him to set himself up as a grocer or a French wine salesman, and the portly fellow was relegated to Rotherhite's least glorious police station: Station 2, Swan Lane. Fortunately, his penmanship was such as to make the calligraphers at Charter House drool with envy; he was entrusted with the transcription of reports, the finalization of monthly statements, and any brief administrative correspondence with Station 1.

He was in his fifties when the purely honorary title of neighborhood secretary came into being.

A superintendent in the administration discovered a twenty-year-old recommendation from Sir Broody in the archives and bestowed the title on Sidney Terence Triggs.

By then, it had been ages since anyone in the limited circle of law enforcement, where he was not entirely unknown, had referred to him by any name other than "Sigma" Triggs.

One of his chiefs, Sergeant Humphrey Basket, prided himself on his Hellenism. He had studied at Cambridge before experiencing some setbacks that remained obscure, and he persevered in viewing the *Anabasis*[2] as the one document of adventure and weaponry worthy of surviving the millennia.

Basket assigned him the patronymic initials of S. T. Triggs in Greek and named him Sigma-Tau-Triggs.

Over the years, the "Tau" fell away and the Sigma remained.

Triggs adopted it without argument and even, if one believes a certain hot story told at Rotherhite's Station 2 that would give rise to laughter, took some pride in it.

Required to recite, during testimony before the Judge of the Old Bailey, his titles and qualifications, he proudly declared: Sigma Triggs, Constable of Her Gracious Majesty.

At the age of fifty he was still to be found in his accustomed place in Swan Lane: plump, rosy, and smiling; his gumball nose, thin gold glasses, and an oddly crafted jacket with padded hips made him look like a Pickwick[3] in petticoats, crudely enlarged via a pantograph.

This office was dark and suffused with tallow, where the gas was turned on at two o'clock in the afternoon, looking onto the high walls of the warehouses of "Learoyd and Larkins," and from where one could estimate the immediate vicinity of the *River*'s tragic waters.

In this cubbyhole reeking of the oily ink of rubber stamps, the sulfurous acid of pyritic charcoal smoking in the tin stove, and the sweat of Sigma Triggs, the latter experienced the only police adventures of his life. There were two.

One morning, as he was beginning his shift, two bobbies brought him a friendly drunkard who had been found sleeping in a nearby warehouse and who had refused to comply with the orders of the wardens who wanted him to vacate the premises as soon as possible.

"Mr. Triggs," requested one of the officers, "Sergeant Basket is very busy at the moment and asks if you would take this fellow's statement."

This was normal. The Rotherhite stations had been ordered to focus, to the full extent possible, on reports of the prowlers and river pirates infesting the area, for possible cleanup expeditions.

Sigma Triggs took pleasure in this work which was being entrusted to him for the first time.

Usually, the attendants in this service employed a reasonable haste, and the "medium noses," "oval faces," "special features: none" were the price paid for these written portraits that no one consulted.

But Sigma Triggs gave it the attention of a neophyte. He meticulously described the drunkard's smirk, examined with a magnifying glass a small V-shaped scar above the left eye, and he even rescued from oblivion an old caliper with wooden sliders to take the man's measurements.

The latter, who at first willingly lent himself to these maneuvers, and even commented on them with a degree of humor, began to show concern. He embarked on an interminable and confused story to explain the presence of the scar.

"The cap' should take care not to write that it's from birth, since it was caused by a fall on the docks of the Pool,[4] an accident at which two or three honorable gentlemen were present who can testify under oath. So the cap' should take care to avoid any confusion..."

Sigma Triggs was no police captain; he thought only of the thickness and thinness of the Englishman's face, and a variation of a twentieth of a millimeter in the regularity of some quotation marks was enough to cost him a sleepless night, but the drunkard's manner struck him as peculiar.

He stunned Humphrey Basket by asking him to authorize his absence for a few hours and to keep the fellow he had just written up under lockdown.

For the first and last time in his life, Sigma Triggs ascended the wide bluestone stairs of Scotland Yard.

He sailed from office to office, resisted the rebuffs of the bailiffs, aroused the malicious curiosity of the orderly officers, and finally ended up, all in a sweat, in the archives.

Two hours later he arrived breathless at Swan Street station and, before justifying his unusual absence, asked for a tall glass of water.

So it was that he spoke plainly to Humphrey Basket, who was looking at him with round saucer eyes:

"Well, here you go, Sergeant: the fellow I've picked up is Bunny Smauker, Barnes's killer, who's been on the run for over seven years. I found his portrait in the archives of Scotland Yard; the small V-shaped scar is very visible there."

Bunny Smauker was tried and hanged; his last words were aimed at Sigma Triggs, whom he called a dirty copper, a snitch, and an assassin.

Before setting foot on the fatal trapdoor, he vowed to return from the Hereafter and haunt his nights by tugging on his toes. Sigma Triggs received an official reward of one hundred pounds and another of five hundred pounds which had been promised by the parents of Smauker's victims. He added this considerable increase to his already plump bank account, for he was thrifty and quite close with his pennies.

From the second adventure, Sigma Triggs derived less fame and profit.

One evening, as he was neatly returning pens, rulers, and pencils to his desk and thinking of the approaching joy of his solitary evening grog, a violent commotion broke out in the adjoining office. Heavy objects battered the walls and doors, chairs were overturned, curses and cries of anger erupted.

Triggs shook off his adipose inertia and sprang forward.

It was just in time: Humphrey Basket, struggling with a tall fellow, had just rolled on the floor, banging his head against the grate of the hearth.

Sigma threw himself with all his weight on the attacker and administered a significant thrashing, but the bandit combined flexibility with vigor.

Triggs suddenly felt an iron hand squeeze his neck and, as he was freeing himself, a hook to his chin knocked him out.

When Basket came to, he congratulated his secretary nonetheless.

"By Jove, Sigma, without your intervention this rascal would have incurred the cost of a first-class burial for the Metropolitan Police Administration for a public servant who died in the line of duty. I have escaped, but so has Mike Sloop."

"Mike Sloop, the forger?"

"In person, my boy; he would have made a fine catch for Station 2, which is not used to such windfalls, but I'm afraid he will continue to be on the run."

So it went; Mike Sloop was no longer under arrest, and Sigma Triggs had to endure the hook, with no hope of repaying it on that crook's sinister face.

With that, Sigma Triggs reached the age of fifty-five and completed the thirty years of good and loyal service which qualified him for retirement.

He hesitated to take it; he still lacked a few hundred pounds of the capital he had always wanted to reach before going to live in the country.

"Well, five more years to go at Rotherhite," he told himself, "and I'll be where I always wanted to be."

He remained there less than six months.

Sir Broody passed away in his nineties at his Ingersham estate, and his will showed that he had never forgotten his former protégé.

He bequeathed to him, in addition to two thousand five hundred pounds, free of all taxes, a pretty house in the main square of Ingersham, expressing the hope that his dear Sidney Terence Triggs would occupy it himself.

It was a wish, not an order; nonetheless, Sigma Triggs decided to comply.

In truth, he didn't care for London, which had always seemed to him hostile, sordid, and much too large.

He had few memories of Ingersham, where he had spent a brief portion of his childhood; but the thought of finishing out his life in the expansive calm of a tiny town on the borders of Middlesex and Surrey did not displease him.[5]

He retired, verifying his pension accounts in minute detail to confirm that he would receive the maximum benefits, found himself satisfied, and turned his back on Rotherhite and London, with neither regret nor joy.

He showed no emotion until Humphrey Basket gave him, by way of a souvenir, a curious little Malaysian warclub that he held very dear.

"As a token of my friendship, and as a remembrance of the day you kept my own head from being broken," said the sergeant.

"I will write to you!" Sigma promised.

Indeed, he wrote to him, though only once . . . But that's getting ahead of ourselves . . .

In the thirty years that Triggs spent in London, he moved only twice. For the last twenty years he had lived in a grim three-room apartment on Marden Street with the Widow Croppins.

This lady, who like all boardinghouse keepers had seen better days, supplemented her meager hostess income by fortune-telling for the ladies in the neighborhood.

She predicted the future with cards, the Egyptian tarot, coffee grounds, and King Henry's candle clock, and claimed to be skilled in geomancy. She boasted of descending straight from the famous Red Nixon,[6] who enjoyed a true prophet's glory at the turn of the last century, and she was said to hold some of his formidable secrets.

The day Bunny Smauker was hanged high and tight in Pentonville Prison,[7] Mrs. Croppins knocked over a lamp during one of her sessions and the fire scorched three cards of her tarot.

She saw it as an omen worth studying.

As the consulted tarot remained silent, she made recourse to geomancy, and the handful of sand, removed at night from a cemetery mound, told her, through certain unusual forms, that a ghost was about to prowl around her home.

She immediately traced the magic pentagram in charcoal on all the western walls of the rooms because there is nothing that unclean spirits breaking free from their eternal hell find more frightening.

Sigma Triggs, who was a man of order and little imagination, declined the protective emblem; not that he was averse to such devotions on the side, based on the simplest of superstitions, but the sooty pentagram offended his aesthetic sensibilities.

With a swipe of his washcloth, he removed it from the walls of his room.

That night he was roused from sleep by three muffled blows at the head of his bed and, in a ray of moonlight filtering through the badly joined curtains, he witnessed a weird pendulum swinging in front of the chandelier.

Sigma Triggs grabbed a cane he used for chasing rats, those stubborn guests of the Marden Street house, and struggled in vain against a misty, hostile shadow swaying three feet above the ground.

He didn't say anything to Mrs. Croppins, but he admitted that Bunny Smauker had kept his hideous oath.

He disdained the aid of the pentagram, in which he hardly believed, but he hastened his preparations for departure.

He would have liked to consult his friend Humphrey Basket, but he had much to do in those days.

The administration had blamed him for Mike Sloop's escape and exacted sweet revenge.

Sloop was accused, rightly or wrongly, of putting counterfeit ten-shilling coins and even one-pound notes in circulation which were so well made that they circulated shamelessly throughout the metropolis.

Basket set out on the trail of the man who had escaped his clutches, and though he focused on nothing else, he was unable to recapture him.

Triggs suspected that a policeman, busy as Basket was now, would not have cared much for ghost stories.

Twice more he inflicted an inconsequential caning on the writhing ghost, then quickly packed his trunks, declined Mrs. Croppins's offer of a farewell supper, paid her a quarter's rent, along with a royal tip for the solitary scullion, and took the coach for Ingersham, a small town forgotten by the railroad's progress that made no complaint thereof.

☙❧

Ingersham baffles the uninformed visitor by looking more like a village in Flanders than a town in Middlesex or Surrey; it seems more the construction of the creators of Épinal prints[8] than that of urban architects.

A large main square, all in hard lines and bright colors due to the variously tinted facades, a few old houses with steps and gables helmed in wicker, a lovely church with a steeple as sharp as a schoolboy's pencil, whose incumbent no longer resides in Ingersham but a league away in Lorking, and a splendid city hall dating from the early fourteenth century.

This building of dark and grandiose art, enormous and massive, crushes the frail houses crammed in its sovereign shadow with its haughty majesty. Its past is rich in historical memories: Chaucer took refuge there before fleeing to Flanders; Elizabeth, the virgin queen, wove and unraveled dark intrigues; Cromwell sat there amidst the Roundheads and sacrificed a few dozen stubbornly royalist inhabitants to the bloody appetites of the day; on its large bluestone square, Puritan fanaticism lit the stake for the papists; and for a century, witches, necromancers, and cabalists died there in torment, much to the chagrin of their demonic master.

On the other hand, if one measures the main square by the acre, the streets, which end there like rivers into the sea, are narrow and penumbral.

Their houses have little green windows hung with muslin; the grocery stores are lit by petrol and even by candlelight; the cabarets, actually few in number, have low ceilings made of dense Caledonian oak and smell of sour ale and fresh rum.

Returning to the main square and facing the west, we find a line of fairly comfortable shops in the following order:

The haberdashery of the Pumkins ladies, where, in addition to stiff fabrics and hard laces, peppermint and anise candies and chocolate papillotes are sold; even—according to certain malicious tongues—sweet liqueurs were served to customers.

Freemantle's butcher shop, known for its veal and ham pâtés, its larded legs of lamb and Midlands-style sausages, with pink flesh flavored with coarse pepper, thyme, and marjoram.

The bakery and pastry shop of jovial Revinus, undisputed master of puddings, cakes, muffins, scones, rich darioles, cinnamon waffles, Italian marzipan with pistachios.

The grand mansion, with its endless facade pierced by twenty-five arched windows, of the Mayor of Ingersham, the Honorable Mr. Chadburn.

The Cobwell Department Store laid out and organized, according to its owner, Mr. Gregory Cobwell, like the department stores in London and Paris, where everything is for sale, especially the dust that constantly accumulates on that mishmash of merchandise.

Mr. Theobald Pycroft's drugstore, which smells of valerian a hundred paces away and attracts every cat in the area.

Past the Pycroft drugstore, the line of facades is cut with a knife and gives way to a vast green space, the beginning of the dark, damp parkland of Sir Broody's immense property.

The house Sigma Triggs inherited stood across the plaza from this opulent array of stone buildings, its windows facing north.

It adjoined with houses of much lesser rank: the widow Pilcarter's puny confectionery to the right and, to the left, forming the corner of an alley leading across fields toward Ingersham's moor, the Peully, the painter Slumbot's workshop.

The rest of the houses grouped in a circle around the city hall and the church are not important enough for me to devote even a few lines to them.

They shelter the calm life of a few rentiers painfully eating into their farthings, or are small clientele shops and café-restaurants whose few visitors sit down to inexpensive drinks and Lenten menus.

Triggs's house had once been rented, at a very low cost, to Doctor Skipper, a health officer who had rendered good and loyal service to Sir Broody.

The kindly quack thought he was doing a work of gratitude by bequeathing, after his death, his furniture and objects of art—very beautiful indeed—to his benefactor.

Sir Broody did not know what to do with all of this and left the house as it was; as a result, Sigma Triggs made his entry as owner, not to an empty house, but to a well-furnished one, as comfortable as one could wish, and ready to make his life as pleasant as possible.

The caretakers were an old couple, the Snipgrasses, living in a doll's house at the far end of the garden where they were happy and content with their lot.

They declared themselves delighted to enter Triggs's service and to not have to vacate premises which had become dear to their simple servant souls.

"Finally," said Mr. Triggs to himself, settling down in a deep Voltaire armchair and stuffing his pipe with coarse Ouse tobacco, "for the first time in my life, I'm at home."

On leaving London he had bought on sale from a bookseller in Paternoster Row the complete works of Dickens illustrated by Reynolds.

At first he amused himself by looking at the pictures and as he found some of the characters likeable, he began reading them, starting with the adventures of Nicholas Nickleby.

He had decided to live a bit of the hermit's life, unaware that small towns often decide otherwise.

Visitors soon roused him from his repose; the mayor summoned him to his office under an administrative pretext and, learning that he had been part of the metropolitan police, immediately bestowed upon him the title of superintendent.

"A former superintendent of Scotland Yard . . . What an honor for Ingersham!"

The spark of pride, which sleeps in all souls, awakened in that of Sigma Triggs, who did not reject the praise.

A week later he made his major and minor entrances into city hall and into Mr. Chadburn's large and luxurious house.

Soon after, it was the druggist Pycroft's turn to capture the heart of the old loner by sending him an elixir of his own—hadn't he learned that Mr. Triggs, the famous Scotland Yard detective, had a cough?

Sigma Triggs hadn't coughed, but he felt flattered and content nonetheless; he visited Mr. Pycroft and they became friends at once.

The three Pumkins ladies came to the threshold of their haberdashery as he walked along their sidewalk, and they bowed gracefully at him and smiled even more gracefully.

Freemantle bluntly invited him to taste his sausages, and the jovial Revinus reminded him that they had once hunted young magpies together in Sir Broody's park.

Even Mr. Gregory Cobwell, in whom Triggs found a loathsome resemblance to Mr. Squeers, the odious schoolmaster of Greta Bridge,[9] was kind and considerate to him, giving him the run of his dusty shops and offering him a glass of blackberry wine that reeked of the weevil . . .

Everyone greeted him, some calling him "captain," and others "inspector."

"We'll sleep easier now, with a man like that within our walls," they said—and some believed it.

Alas! . . .

☙

Having completed our review of Ingersham's notables, we should not altogether neglect the humble folk.

Especially since Sigma Triggs became very attached to one of them, the gentle Mr. Ebenezer Doove.

Ingersham's city hall, a building worthy of a city of at least 60,000 souls, could easily have been replaced by a modest town hall with three or four offices and a guard room. This colossus of gray stone contained about thirty rooms, of which six or seven were of considerable size, an archival gallery where the layman wanders as in a forest, and endless underground passages and attics capable of housing a regiment.

Mr. Chadburn, who was a great visionary and felt cramped living in a house with fewer than seven balconies and three dining rooms, could not condemn three-quarters of his city hall to deserted loneliness. Therefore, he had not hesitated to engage in a veritable hiring binge of unnecessary staff, whom he paid mostly with his own money.

Bailiffs paced the echoing corridors without encountering anyone throughout the eight hours of their required presence; four scribes languished for the same number of hours before the nearly blank civil status registers; half a dozen boys moved, aimlessly and without purpose, from room to room; three old men were dying of boredom in the solemn dust of the archives, while idle secretaries munched on their pencils and pen holders in the hollow peace of the extensive official offices.

Among those pointless desks, Sigma Triggs wasted no time in making a friend. At the end of the immense waiting hall where paintings by Flemish and German masters were yellowing, under an immense and sooty canvas by Hildebrandt,[10] in a large glass cage bearing the sign "Information," an old clerk with hunched shoulders, his lifeless eyes protected by tinted glasses, tirelessly blackened large white sheets with administrative headers.

Mr. Ebenezer Doove was, however, of quite some use, as he worked without respite for the past glory of Ingersham.

He had provided commentary, in a 120-page brochure, on a statement of communal accounts including the costs of the occupation, residence, justice, and reception of Oliver Cromwell and his henchmen.

He had discovered twelve leaves of a *sotie*,[11] which he attributed to Ben Jonson, and had completed it in his own hand until it grew into a substantial work of two hundred closely written pages.

Having found in the ledger of an inn where Southey[12] had stayed for eight days, "At the Arms of Chatham," an establishment that had since disappeared, he generously signed this great name to seven brief anonymous poems, written in green ink in an old album of poetry taken from the municipal archives.

Mr. Doove, to whom the administration and Mr. Chadburn granted modest emoluments, amplified them by writing petitions for the eternal beggars of royal or other favors, by drafting protests and claims for taxpayers mistreated by the tax authorities, and elaborating tender missives for the use of lovers confused by spelling and the art of beautiful sentences.

By chance, one of these epistles fell into the hands of Sigma Triggs; it didn't interest him much, and he even found it a little ridiculous; but he was struck with admiration for the finely formed writing, the harmonious order of words and their intervals.

He knew no rest until he had met this man whom he deemed at the time to be of good taste and great talent.

Doove confided in him that he had a specimen of the handwriting of William Chickenbroker, who in his time was the king's calligrapher and had partially transcribed Smollett's *History of England*.[13]

It didn't take more than that to quickly cement a solid friendship of mutual esteem between the two men.

Ebenezer Doove soon became familiar with the Triggs home; he was all the more welcome since he had once secured a modest disabled veteran's pension for old Snipgrass through dogged and skillful correspondence.

Doove and Triggs, united by a love of the beautiful written form, found a common liking for lamb stew with shallots, lemon grog, and beer toddy.

And it was Mr. Doove who, in an expansive hour, revealed a great secret to his new friend.

"I would not confide it to anyone else: the honorable Mr. Chadburn would wish me dead, and half the inhabitants of Ingersham would call me a liar or a daydreamer, if not a madman, while a mighty terror would render the other half unable to eat or drink," said the old scribe.

"Hey!" cried Mr. Triggs. "Is it really that serious?"

"Serious? Hm . . . it's a question of interpretation. I myself, having read and even commented on Shakespeare a bit, adopt Hamlet's dark words: 'There are more things in heaven and earth, than are dreamt of in your philosophy.' Do you understand?"

"Eh . . . yes, no doubt," replied Sigma Triggs, who in fact did not understand at all.

"You are a renowned detective, Mr. Triggs, and as such you must adopt a hardheaded and skeptical attitude."

"No doubt, no doubt," repeated Sigma, who understood less and less where the old man was coming from.

The notary's pale hands twitched slightly.

"I will tell you then, Mr. Triggs: there is a ghost in city hall!"

This time, the former secretary of the Rotherhite post did indeed cough; he had, in fact, plunged the stem of his pipe deep into his throat.

"Im . . . impossible!" he stammered, his eyes full of tears.

"It's a fact!" Mr. Doove asserted forcefully.

"Impossible!" said Mr. Triggs more forcefully.

But inwardly he called himself a liar; he had just thought of the noose swinging in the moonlight in his room on Marden Street.

II

Mr. Doove Tells Some Stories

Humphrey Basket had not received the confidences of his subordinate, and not a day went by without the latter regretting it. It seemed to him that the inspector's quiet voice, clear eyes, and sober demeanor would have made short shrift of the specter that haunted his lonely nights.

The burden of the invisible weighed too heavily on his heart, and he couldn't wait to find someone to whom he could pass on part of it in confidence.

He had hesitated between Mr. Chadburn, the merry Revinus, and even the simple Snipgrasses; but now he had found a true soulmate in the very understanding Mr. Doove.

A man possessing a text in the elegant hand of William Chickenbroker, who valued, above all else, the immutable splendor of handwriting, could only lend him an attentive ear, perhaps even provide him with advice.

One evening, before a particularly well-prepared grog, accompanied by the copious smoke of Dutch pipes, he told the story of Bunny Smauker, of Mrs. Croppins's apprehension, the protective pentagrams, and finally the sinister phantom pendulum.

Ebenezer Doove did not laugh incredulously. He blamed neither his friend's nerves nor his imagination. He thought deeply as he drew heavy puffs from his pipe.

One should expect no less from a man who gravely asserts the existence of a specter in an official building; nonetheless, he did not add on the gloomy refrain, and he even omitted further mention of his own ghost in support of the disquisition that Mr. Triggs awaited.

He simply whispered, his eyes lost in the blue haze of tobacco: "We'll have to see . . . Yes, we'll have to see."

It was only a week later, after an interesting exchange of views on the addition of certain Gothic characters in the transcription of some ceremonial pieces, that he said abruptly:

"My dear Triggs, I am convinced that you are not a seer, and I in turn flatter myself that I am not one either. It is impossible to offer a so-called rational explanation of certain phenomena that provoke boundless amazement and often the most abject of terrors.

"I want to tell you in turn a true story, all the more truthful in that I lived it and that its memory remains fixed in every fiber of my being.

"It is said that every self-respecting Englishman believes in a ghost at least once in his life; I know many of our compatriots, however, who are irreducibly incredulous when it comes to things from the Beyond.

"They are wrong, and I proclaim it without doubt. I told you about the Ghost of City Hall; that's a different story than today's, and if I tell it to you one day, I'll do it my way, which is to say, I'll try to put it to you, not through words that depict the past thing, but through tangible facts of the present."

Here, Sigma Triggs shivered slightly; one ghost had been enough for him, and he had vaguely hoped to see Mr. Doove blow out his fright like noxious smoke.

Ebenezer Doove ended the preamble and began:

"I had gotten lost in the fog. A fog like I have never seen since, even in London on foggy days: a real damp and yellowish tow, stinking of the mud of the nearby swamps.

"Did I tell you this was in Ireland, on the banks of the Shannon? During the day, I had visited a town with historical artifacts from the eighteenth century, which I had studied—alas, in vain!—in calligraphic manuscripts, written in variously colored inks, and I expected to be back in Limerick by dusk.

"I had rented a bicycle which was not very sturdy and whose chain had come loose; nevertheless, by sparing it a little, I could have made the return trip, save for that damned fog.

"But the cursed chain had something of the devil about it, because it came completely loose when the fog lifted.

"I had to bring myself to push my bike by hand.

"I then saw that I was on a kind of grassy track winding through water-soaked moorland interspersed with oaks and dwarf privet.

"This respite didn't last long; immense clouds rose on the horizon fringed with ashes and smoke; the wind began to blow in gusts and a hellish rain fell.

"Half a mile from me stood a grassy knoll, a kind of greenish hill to which I headed to make an observation post from whence I could recognize the surroundings and, God knows, discover a refuge conducive to my poor person soaked to the bone.

"My nose had served me well: I found a refuge there.

"It was a single-story country house, surrounded by a desolate little park, and separated from the grassy track, which must have led to it, by a wrought-iron gate.

"Through the resonant curtain of the rain, I saw the reflection of a fire behind one of the windows on the ground floor, and this flame immediately came to represent for me the brightness of a haven.

"I pushed the recalcitrant bicycle more actively and reached the gate just as a violent thunderclap shook the space.

"I looked for the button or the foot switch of a doorbell in vain: there was none, but the gate was not closed and all I needed was a turn of the handle to open it.

"Thirty paces away, the fire danced madly, stirring shadows and red lights; I headed for the window and tried to see inside.

"I saw only a tall chimney in which a fire of dry gorse and stumps was burning; the rest of the room, which seemed spacious to me, was shrouded in darkness.

"You may be sopping wet and hear lightning strike two hundred yards behind you, but you still observe proprieties; I knocked on the dusty windows.

"After what seemed like a very long time, I heard the sound of footsteps; the door, which was on the far side of the housefront, opened, and I saw a livid head lean out for a moment.

"'May I come in?' I asked.

"The head instantly disappeared, but the door remained open.

"The rain intensified with such rage that I began to run and, pushing my bicycle in front of me, I rushed into the corridor.

"The door to the room was open and I saw the scarlet light of the flames reflecting vividly on the walls.

"These were in a terrible state of decrepitude: cracks the width of a thumb streaked the flaking plaster and the passage of slugs was inscribed everywhere in silver ribbons. I set my machine against one of the walls and bravely entered the room.

"It was dirty and bare, containing only a half-smashed table, two crumbling stools, and, truly surprisingly, a magnificent armchair of cordovan leather pulled as close as possible to the fire. That's where I settled down, my feet on the rusty andirons, my hands outstretched toward the flames.

"I may not have closed the door, but the truth is that I neither saw nor heard the master of the house enter. I found him standing beside my chair without my being able to say how he came to be there.

"I then saw the most singular creature I had ever met; he was an old man, but so lean, so slender, that it was almost impossible for such a being to survive. He was dressed in a long frock coat that fell almost to his feet, and he held his long and diaphanous hands entwined as if in prayer.

"But what was most extraordinary about him was his head. It was snow-white and absolutely bald. For a moment I was afraid to look into his eyes, expecting to find them frightful in such a face; but they were completely closed, and I realized that the man was blind.

"I began immediately to tell him how I had arrived at his home: the reluctant bicycle, the fog, the rain, the storm.

"He remained motionless, seeming not to hear or listen to me, and had it not been for a slight senile trembling of his head, I would have taken him for an ugly and fantastic statue.

"I no longer expected to hear a voice rise from that hollow chest, nor words fall from those barely visible lips, when he suddenly spoke in a very low tone, though in the language of one raised as a gentleman.

"'It's a long way from here to Dublin,' he said.

"'I'm not going to Dublin, but to Limerick,' I said.

"My answer seemed to plunge him into a strange confusion.

"'Please don't be offended,' he whispered.

"His hands separated and a long arm shot up close to my face; I then felt his fingers brush my neck, feel it, then withdraw in terror.

The singular and painful contact! The touch of his fingers had more the effect on me of a current of icy air than that of a material body.

"'You are no doubt sitting in the armchair?' he asked.

"'Certainly . . . Do you wish for me to leave it?'

"'No, no, but when night comes, it might be wise for you to take a seat on one of the stools.'

"He turned around and I saw him approach a cupboard with disjointed doors, from which he took out a bottle and placed it on the table.

"'You may help yourself,' he said.

"He walked to the door, opened it, and I saw him no longer.

"I was cold and the bottle tempted me.

"It contained one of the finest Spanish wines I have ever drunk; I did so without letting the bottle touch my lips and emptied half of it.

"Then, overcome by the generous drink, the cozy warmth of the fire, and my fatigue, I fell asleep in the comfortable armchair.

"In the middle of the night, I was suddenly awakened.

"The fire was still burning, but less brightly; nevertheless, it projected enough light that I could see around the room. Nobody was there; however, my memory returning, I realized that I had been roused from my sleep by a violent shove, the pain of which I still felt.

"I thought of the bottle and reached for it; at the same moment, it was pushed away, without my being able to say why or how, and thrown angrily against the ground where it broke.

"I leaned back in the chair; immediately I was seized by the neck, lifted up like a common rabbit, and thrown into the middle of the room.

"I got up, both scared and angry.

"Then the chair groaned as if someone were sitting in it, and I heard a deep sigh.

"Why am I stubborn? The truth is that I felt terribly offended by what had just happened. I walked over to the chair wanting to sit down again.

"Well ... *someone was sitting in the chair*. Someone I did not see, but who made his presence known to me.

"I was grabbed with extreme fury, shaken violently, and thrown over the table against the door.

"That did it for me. At this point, I had become a man absolutely bereft of cold reason, horrified beyond belief.

"I rushed into the hallway, grabbed my bicycle, and pushed it outside.

"Through some sort of magic I managed to fix the chain in no time at all, and with the aid of this same magic—unless it were all the good saints of Ireland—through storm, downpour, and hurricane, I arrived in Limerick at the first light of day.

"I had a few friends in that town, and one of them, Dr. O'Neil, seemed to me a man worth confiding in.

"He listened to me without interrupting, his forehead lined with wrinkles.

"'I know this house,' he said finally. 'It is that of the Kairnes family; it has been completely abandoned for five years.'

"'But the fire, the armchair, the wine, and above all the pale man! ...' I exclaimed, annoyed and irritated.

"'I have only one answer for you,' said the doctor. 'The blind man you have just described to me and who is known to me is Joseph Sumbroë, the old servant of the Kairnes; only he died five years ago.'

"I let out an exclamation of anger and horror.

"'And the last of the Kairnes, a boy gone bad, a formidable creature, a giant nearly seven feet tall and as strong as a tiger, had burdened his conscience with several murders, all carried out in the most horrible manner. He was hanged yesterday.'

"As I was silent, mute with horror, the doctor continued:

"'However, I seem to understand the strange adventure that was yours this night. The pale man told you it's a long way from here to Dublin. And he thought you were James Kairnes, the last of his masters.'

"'But that's not an explanation!' I exclaimed.

"'No doubt, but it is the only one I can think of; I am sorry if it leads you to sneer and call me an old woman: the shade of the old and faithful servant waiting for the shade of his last master in the house that belonged to him, and the shade of the dead man, fierce, returning to find you installed in his place and receiving you as he did.'"

... M. Doove fell silent and, after a moment of silence, finished: "Here ends my story."

For once, Mr. Triggs felt a sort of revolt rise within him.

"Come, come, Mr. Doove, now tell me that you later discovered that the ghostly servant was an impostor, and that he had you drink drugged wine, which gave you a dreadful nightmare."

The old man nodded gravely.

"Alas, my friend, the detective speaks in you! I found nothing like that, and everything Dr. O'Neil told me was true.

"However, I behaved like a reasonable man, in love with holy and sound logic; provided with a recommendation from my friend the doctor, I went the same day to Dublin where I was authorized to see the corpse of the victim, who had not yet been buried in his shroud of quicklime.

"He was a terrible creature, with the muzzle of a gorilla and enormous hands; even in death he looked so fearsome that the mortuary guards turned away in horror."

"And the house?" whispered Mr. Triggs.

"Here also, I saw rising before me an insurmountable barrier to any investigation. In the course of the terrifying night, lightning had struck it, reducing it completely to ashes."

"Goodness!" moaned Mr. Triggs.

Mr. Doove emptied his glass of toddy and refilled his pipe.

"And I can only repeat the words of our great Will: There are more things in heaven and earth..."

They relinquished the subject for some time; it was Sigma Triggs who returned to it, although he had promised himself not to.

"Hanged men seem to enjoy returning to earth," he said one evening, receiving his friend at his table.

He had tried to give an ironic turn to his words, but in reality, he was sweating with fear.

Mr. Doove replied, with his customary gravity: "I am a bit of a bookdealer. Oh, very little, because my means are limited—but I discovered, at a scrap dealer in Paternoster Row, a very curious little treatise, published by Reeves and written by a stranger who signed his work 'Adelbert' followed by three asterisks. Were it not for the testimonials and the marginal quotations, I would be inclined to treat this work as a bit of macabre literary humbug.

"But, as I have just had the good fortune of telling you, the testimonials appeared quite solid to me and the notes indisputably authentic.

"After numerous examples, most as funereal as the others, where it was a question of more or less malevolent ghosts of torture victims, and especially of hanged men, the author concluded: *It seems that beyond the gibbet a vestigial life remains to the victims of execution, a life they devote to the obscure work of revenge against those who led them to the scaffold.*

"*They haunt the sleep of their judges and of the police servants who contributed to their capture; they appear, even in broad daylight, while their victims are awake.*

"*Many of the latter have sunk into madness or have preferred suicide to a life eternally threatened with the worst nightmares.*

"*Some even died in mysterious ways, in which a criminal hand not of this world is believed to be at work.*"[1]

"Well, I never! . . ." said Sigma Triggs, barely breathing.

"If you are particularly interested, I can share with you the story of Judge Cruyshank of Liverpool, in the year 1846."[2]

"Tell it!" agreed Triggs, his heart sinking.

"Let's see, let me remember what this Adelbert of the three stars has to say about it. Ah! here it is: 'Harmon Cruyshank justly deserved the reputation of a judge who was honest, but severe. In the name of justice, he knew no pity.

"'He had to judge the case of William Burbank, a young man who, during a drunken brawl, killed one of his friends.

"'Harmon Cruyshank donned the black cap when the fatal "Guilty" sentence was handed down and pronounced the death warrant without emotion: ". . . Condemned to hang by the neck until dead." Then these words fell from his dry lips: "May God have mercy on your poor soul!"

"'Young Burbank fixed him with a terrible look: "But God will never have mercy on yours, and that I will vouch for."

"'The murderer walked bravely to his execution and the judge forgot him. Not for long though; one morning, as Harmon Cruyshank was getting ready to go out, he took a last look in the mirror, for he demanded of himself impeccable dress, and he saw a rope swinging in the mirror's depths.

"'He turned around, believing the reflection a real thing, but soon realized that the rope only existed in the glass.

"'The next day, at the same time, he saw it again; but this time a slipknot adorned the end.

"'Harmon Cruyshank thought it was a hallucination and consulted a renowned psychiatrist, who advised him to seek rest, fresh air, exercise, and a proper diet.

"'For a fortnight, the mirrors fulfilled their straightforward mission as faithful reproducers of images. Then suddenly the phantom cord reappeared.

"'Now the noose was resting on the shoulders of Cruyshank's reflection.

"'After a reassuring eclipse of several weeks, the end came, brutal and horrible.

"'As Cruyshank looked at himself in the mirror, he saw the familiar scenery sink into the depths of the world of reflections. A white haze arose and filled the optical space with an opaque mist.

"'Slowly the spectral cloud dissipated, and the judge saw a narrow prison yard with a gibbet.

"'The executioner finished binding the condemned man's hands and put his own hand on the lever of the fatal trapdoor.

"'With a cry of horror, Cruyshank tried to flee: he had just recognized William Burbank in the sinister person of the executioner and his own image in that of the man destined for a disgraceful death.

"'He could not make a move; he saw the trapdoor open and his double slip into the void.

"'Harmon Cruyshank was found dead in front of a mirror showing only its innocent and customary reflections; he had been strangled, and his neck bore the white mark of the deadly hemp.'"

ᘳᘰᘬ

Ebenezer Doove told these stories on a radiant summer evening, continuing through to the softness of the stars, the rising moon, and the strident joy of the crickets. Although the atmosphere of mist, rain, and wind was lacking, Mr. Triggs was nonetheless impressed.

The next day, he was still thinking about it, despite the sun and the deep azure of the sky.

The day was hot; the sun, leaving its zenith slowly, set the celestial vastness ablaze.

In the spacious living room that took up much of the first floor of his house, Mr. Triggs, restless despite the heat, paced up and down, breathing heavily.

Through the windows overlooking the garden he could see in the distance, above the withered hedges, the Pompeian green meadows of the Peully; fierce-headed Surrey horses pranced there, indifferent to the furnace blast, and they needed only to rush headlong, horn into the breeze, to be unicorns.

On the luminous water of a canal, barges stretched their sails in the three o'clock sun.

One could hear, in the garden enclave, the hens taking their dust baths, clucking plaintively.

Triggs turned his back on this radiant solitude to gaze out the street windows at the main square, bisected by a ribbon of molten asphalt. The sweltering heat glued fat Revinus to the blue threshold of his shop. The city hall was dressed in luscious gold like a pâté straight from the bakery, and the facades of the houses opposite had taken on the hues of vinous lacquer.

Suddenly, Sigma shut his eyes, pained by a violent ray of sunlight that was projected from the back of the Cobwell Department Store.

"Ah, small-town life!" he grumbled, "you take what fun you can get . . . That idiot Cobwell's enjoying himself with a bit of mirror, shining little suns into people's eyes!"

Sigma Triggs knew nothing of the subtle and disturbing theory of the subconscious. At least his didn't tell him anything.

Nothing of the terror encompassed by this mischievous little game, which had blinded him for a couple of seconds.

III

Games of the Sun and the Moon

When Mr. Gregory Cobwell affirmed that his department store was organized like those of London and Paris, no one dreamed of contradicting him. The people of Ingersham, dedicated homebodies, cared nothing for London, and none of them knew Paris. They were most satisfied with this organization and with the shop itself where, at the cost of some patience, one always managed to discover what one wanted: a tortoiseshell comb, a porcelain shaving brush, a yard of flannelette, hair clippers, or thoughtful Valentine's Day cards.

Mr. Cobwell was alone in directing this establishment that was stuffed like the gizzard of a python, and alone in serving the customers, for one could not properly rank Mrs. Chisnutt among the staff, given that she only devoted a couple of hours three times a week to a semblance of cleaning. Nor could one count the lovely Suzan Summerlee.

Physically, Mr. Cobwell was a little man, dark and dry as a cricket, with dull eyes eaten away by blepharitis and a heart weary from asthma, but this did not slow down the antlike activity he put into overturning, lifting, and shifting a chaotic heap of rubbish.

The son of an architect who made his fortune by raising a city of slums on the formerly fallow lands of Houndsditch and Millwall, Gregory Cobwell had dreamed of adding glory to wealth.

He attended a design school in Kensington and gained fame there by writing a pamphlet injurious to the memory of the great Wren,[1] and vague commentaries on the obscure Vitruvius.[2]

But luck turned its back on this swaggering marmoset, for whom the remains of his father's fortune ensured a final mercantile retreat in the quiet haven of Ingersham.

He settled there in stubborn solitude, fiercely celibate despite the undisguised advances of certain ladies in the town; polite and obliging, but nevertheless distant with customers, ignoring others while hating and envying them in his heart.

A singular tenderness was born in this embittered heart for a most singular person: Miss Suzan Summerlee.

This was Cobwell's name for her, for that slender, elegant creature with the face of a Madonna had never had a name, and no one except Gregory Cobwell had thought of giving her one.

He had discovered her one day in the back of a Cheapside up-selling shop where he bought discards at low prices. That day she was wearing a moth-eaten green peplum and red cloth sandals; he acquired them—Miss Suzan, the peplum, and the sandals—for eighteen shillings.

Suzan Summerlee was a chipboard and wax mannequin who had appeared for a few seasons in a fairground show, carrying this sinister sign: *The horrible murderess Pearcy, who killed a man and two children with an axe.*[3]

According to the slanderers, the poor thing looked nothing like the bloody virago, but had featured in an auction lot when a Mayfair clothing store went bankrupt.

Mr. Cobwell installed her in his shops, assigning her the role of dress-up model and mute confidante.

During the long slack hours of the day, he conversed with her, measuring her answers alongside his own:

"So we were saying, Miss Suzan, that Wren ... What? Ha, ha! I see where you're going with this! No, no, say no more, you would get lost on an abominable road. National glory? You speak of Westminster and the many other horrors of stone that dishonor the metropolis. I'm not listening to you anymore, Miss Summerlee: see, I'm stopping my ears. An intelligent and distinguished person such as yourself should not make such mistakes! Believe me, I am sorry. You'll admit that if fortune had deigned to smile on me..."

In the end Miss Suzan Summerlee admitted all that Gregory Cobwell wanted her to, and they got along perfectly.

The little gentleman sometimes sighed when he considered how he might have established himself as a dealer in sugar tongs and bowls, but he consoled himself with the thought that the back of his vast and oversized shop opened into the "Grand Cobwell Art Gallery."

It was a spacious room reached by a staircase of six carpeted steps; acid green draperies and bilious stained glass maintained the atmosphere of a mortuary. With the threshold but barely crossed it proclaimed scabies in all its forms; a composite odor betraying the bedbug, the woodworm, scorched onion, mothballs, and animal urine.

But what did this awful musty smell matter compared to the dazzling misery of this museum of the *caput mortuum*,[4] whose oppressive sadness was obvious to all but Mr. Gregory Cobwell?

Although he had acquired them at extremely low prices, he held the astounding reproductions of French works that covered the walls to be rigorously authentic; the Vernets, the Harpignies, the Ingres, a wretched Fantin-Latour made modest by veils painted on afterward; fake Gobelins, fake Sèvres, Moustiers manufactured in Belgium, and the frosty glassware whose languid whiteness stagnated in the eternal shadow of that place.[5]

An infinite tenderness awakened in the rheum of his gaze before those barbaric groups he attributed to Pigalle and Puget, if not Thorwaldsen or Rodin.[6]

From every angle, he saw spring up, like unheard-of treasures, objects diversely colored, absurd, and grotesque: obscene fetishes from the Islands, grimacing saints from Spain, motheaten fabrics, forms evoking Bruges, Florence, or Cappadocia, an entire flea market of madness that made the gaze jump, powerless to settle on one thing in that surfeit of wretchedness.

With a quivering hand, he caressed, like priceless preciosities, extraordinary objects derived from meager research and destined for clearance sales from their birth. He felt rise within himself a strange pagan piety before the pathetic whiteness of the stucco dryads, huddled in the darkness of their niches.

He had refused to sell a colored plaster model of Durham Cathedral and the miniature of a monochrome wooden dromon next to the frigid mask of an unknown duumvir.[7]

"Miss Summerlee," he would say solemnly, "on certain melancholy evenings, London neglected me, just as I shall neglect London. Ah, I see right through you, my beautiful friend! When I die, you will see this boundless wealth fill the vast space of a room in the British Museum, whose door, lined with protective iron, will bear the inscription: 'The Cabinet of Gregory Cobwell.' Nay, that will never be! All this beauty will not take the road to that most ungrateful city of all!"

He had never revealed his posthumous intentions, and Miss Suzan had never been more curious than usual in this regard.

$\wp$

Gregory Cobwell had finished his solitary meal of purslane salad and fried onions, prepared in a nasty little den he pompously called his "office," and allowed himself a drop of his favorite cordial, a mixture of gin and anisette. After a contemplative pause in front of a sooty canvas by an unknown genius, he had left the art gallery to settle down in front of one of the store's large windows.

Before him lay the shaded part of the main square; it was deserted, for the widow Pilcarter, asleep in a wicker chair on her doorstep, could not be counted as a presence.

The squat silhouette of a dray loaded with cubes of white stone stood out from the facade of a cabaret, where the carters had to wait for a cooler hour to get back on the road.

"Those are Foway[8] stones," said Mr. Cobwell. "They are worth nothing, being soft and crumbly."

He called the impassive Miss Summerlee to witness. Her shining nudity was draped for the moment in a royal blue cape which gave her a grand appearance.

Mr. Cobwell sneered.

"Beautiful and haughty lady, I believe we are once again mistaken. I call the power of optics to my rescue."

In the eyewear department, he picked up a large pair of prismatic binoculars and aimed them over the roof.

"They are Upper Kingston stones, my dear ... Eh, eh! Who, on this sad earth, still claims sufficient genius to employ them according to their value? Our city hall owes two of its most beautiful turrets to them."

Among the works of architecture finding favor in Mr. Cobwell's intolerant eyes was the haughty and somber city hall.

He would often train his binoculars on its crumbling masonry, sigh, and declare that such a monument reconciled him somewhat with the existence which had been imposed on him by fate.

When his attention finally turned away from the dray, he was again solicited by the majestic facade facing him.

"Nice work," he muttered. "I should have lived in that era of greatness."

Suddenly, he gave a slight start.

"Hullo! See there, Miss Suzan, who would still dare claim that the lives of municipal functionaries are idle? Behind that tiny skylight which very rarely attracts my gaze, because it is unwelcome in that stone beauty, I see a busy form moving about."

He meticulously adjusted the prismatic bezel with a few turns of the knobs and went back to observing.

"Just as I said, Miss Summerlee!"

A moment later he exclaimed:

"Let me use the helio-teaser!"[9]

The helio-teaser was this gentleman's personal invention, from which he derived a childish pleasure. It was a small optical device, composed of lenses and a parabolic mirror, which allowed him to send, at a significant distance, circles of sunlight, burning and almost painful, into the eyes of passersby.

"Look, Miss Suzan. With one hand, I hold my binoculars in the direction of the skylight and, with the other, I direct the jet of solar fire from my helio-teaser. Do you understand?"

Miss Summerlee did not say she understood, and Cobwell felt compelled to give her a further explanation.

"The increased clarity will allow me to see into the room opposite, as if I were gluing my eyes to his window, and then I will certainly make that very zealous official jump beneath the slap of the sun from my device. One, two, three . . .

"Oh!"

It was a cry of amazement that arose.

The helio-teaser quivered in the little man's hand, and the ray of sunlight that flew off it roamed other facades and stung Sigma Triggs's eyes.

But Gregory Cobwell had stopped playing. He had dropped the expensive lenses, without any thought of picking them up, and retired to the back of his shop where he sat down on the steps of the art gallery, buried his head in his hands, and began to think.

Sometime later he fetched Miss Summerlee, placed her in the gallery in front of one of the statue niches, and settled himself on the plush sofa beneath a desiccated palm tree.

It was hours before he resumed his soliloquies.

The sun had slowly slid to the west, and a light without heat rose to the roofs of the main square.

The peaceful hour of twilight was approaching; the small bridge that connected the grassy banks of the Greeny had become a large line of shadow, where the silhouette of a man fishing for loach[10] took the form of a shadow puppet.

"Miss Suzan," murmured Cobwell, "you saw it as I did!"

He had raised his head and his frightened eyes went from Suzan to other motionless things less worthy of confidence.

"I can never bear the weight of such a secret!" continued Cobwell, groaning. "What do you think, Miss Suzan?"

The thoughts of the lady in the royal blue mantle were no doubt communicated to him by mysterious means, for he continued:

"A detective has come from London. He is said to be very skilled. These are matters that concern him more than me. But how?"

Miss Suzan's form grew indistinct in the gallery's green shadows.

"Nothing says he didn't come here to uncover that . . . Ah, Miss Summerlee, this time I think you're on the right track! . . . Yes, I'll go find him . . . It's my duty? Are you saying it's my duty? I don't doubt it, don't worry. We're in perfect agreement."

The tranquil whispers of the evening barely penetrated the Cobwell Department Store, where it was already dark; lost in the distance, the voices of a childish roundelay sought to disperse some small joy in a fading world.

Gregory Cobwell thought of years long past when, in a garden on Wood Road, he had known those carefree hours of total bliss, and he sighed:

"I wouldn't be able to sleep, or find any rest," he whimpered. "Do you hear, Suzan? I must find this Mr. Triggs at once!"

Yet he did nothing; powerful suction cups seemed to hold him to the plush couch.

"No one should see me. It will have to be dark, very dark."

This resolution, which led him to delay any action, calmed him somewhat. He got up, went through his regular evening routine mechanically, closed the doors and shutters, and returned to the gallery, which was now lit by a water-lens lamp,[11] to resume his place in front of Miss Summerlee.

"When it's dark . . . dark," he continued, "I assure you I'll go!"

It was very dark, and the lamp he had neglected to fill with oil was rapidly dying out; he did not care, for the moon was rising above the trees in the garden, and its light was already filtering through the drapes. Miss Suzan Summerlee seemed shrouded in silver, and Mr. Cobwell had often delighted in admiring her in her subtle fairy attire.

"No, no," he whispered, "don't think I'll change my mind. I will wait a little longer, though very little, I assure you. Too bad if I have to wake Mr. Triggs from his sleep: a Scotland Yard detective is accustomed to such small annoyances . . . Miss Suzan . . ."

He did not finish this new monologue he intended for his silent friend, but looked at her in amazement.

The shadows and highlights, which rendered her in peculiar reliefs, seemed to become singularly mobile. The green drapes, pierced with moonlight, swelled as if the window behind them had just opened to a draft. Yet Mr. Cobwell knew it was stubbornly closed.

"Miss Suzan . . ."

Now he was not mistaken: it was not only the drapery that moved, but unusual movements animated the lady in the blue mantle. Until then he had looked at her full on; now she presented a three-quarter view, then he saw only her profile, a little hard, a little cruel even.

A silly idea occurred to him: during her spectacular career, Miss Suzan had been known as "Mrs. Pearcy, the horrible axe murderess."

Was it just a vain idea from the past?

Twice, trying to salvage his suddenly faltering sanity, Mr. Cobwell groaned:

"Mistaken identity doesn't count!"

Then he screamed.

It was but a single shrill cry, in which the poor man placed all his horror, his last hope in an improbable help from outside.

Nonetheless, he was heard by Sergeant Lammle, the sole constable ensuring the peace and security of Ingersham.

He was at that moment on the sidewalk of the Cobwell Department Store, his face turned toward the Greeny where he had hoped that night to nab a poacher.

The cry was not repeated, and Lammle said to himself, shrugging his massive shoulders:

"It's just cats!"

Mr. Gregory Cobwell had screamed because he had seen the axe.

But his scream was his last in this world.

꙳

Mrs. Chisnutt, as usual, entered through the garden gate. She had prepared some tea in the pantry, toasted some bread, and rang a big brass bell which was supposed to rouse her master from sleep and announce lunch to him.

She received no answer and went upstairs, where she found herself facing an empty bedroom, in which the bed had not been unmade.

In the art gallery she discovered Mr. Gregory Cobwell and began to howl, for, as she later recounted throughout the town, "He was dreadfully ugly to look at, and his eyes seemed ready to pop out of his head."

Ten minutes later, Mr. Chadburn, the mayor, Apothecary Pycroft, and Sergeant Lammle stood before the corpse.

Another ten minutes passed, and old Dr. Cooper made his entrance, with Mr. Sigma Triggs following at his heels.

In cases he deems serious, a mayor has the right to deputize one or more constables on the spot, and Mr. Chadburn used that authority to install the former police secretary in this role.

"I opt for natural death," declared old Cooper, "but I will not be able to decide formally until after the autopsy."

"Natural death ... Oh yes, no doubt," muttered Mr. Triggs, already relieved of future responsibilities.

"He looks funny," said Sergeant Lammle; then he went back to sucking on his pencil.

"He had a weak heart," said Apothecary Pycroft. "I sometimes sold him tonics."

"I wonder what he could be looking at like that," said Sergeant Lammle. "I mean: what he was looking at before he died."

"What else but that diabolical cardboard creature," growled Mrs. Chisnutt, happy to insert her word. "He only had eyes for this shameless statue; it must, sooner or later, have cried out to heaven for vengeance."

"And to think," murmured Lammle, "that I heard him scream— for I no longer doubt it was him."

"What?" asked Mr. Chadburn.

The sergeant's pencil passed from his mouth into his hair.

"Well, uh ... it's difficult to specify; at first it seemed to me I heard a name, hurled out in a shrill voice, something like Gala ... Gala ... wait, Galantine ... yeah, that's funny, huh? Then a scream and that was it.

"I thought it was some crazy old woman calling her cat followed by what I thought was the tomcat's answer. So."

"He was indeed looking at the mannequin," said Dr. Cooper slowly, "and seldom have I seen an expression of such fear spread over the face of a dead man."

"The devil must have gotten into it," retorted Mrs. Chisnutt. "It wouldn't be so surprising after all."

"Can you die of fright?" asked Mr. Chadburn.

"Certainly, when the shock is violent and one is weakhearted," said Mr. Pycroft.

"The window is open," remarked Mr. Triggs.

"It never is!" cried Mrs. Chisnutt.

"He must have run out of air and hastened to get some," scoffed the apothecary. "Isn't that right, doctor?"

"Uh, probably . . ." concurred the doctor.

Sergeant Lammle had taken a quick tour of the stores and was returning with the prismatic binoculars.

"These were on the ground, in front of the street window," he said, "and they're broken."

"It is an expensive object," remarked Mr. Triggs. "I'm surprised he left it there."

"There was also this," continued the sergeant, handing him the helio-teaser.

Mr. Triggs examined the small device, nodding thoughtfully.

"Well, you don't have to be a great scholar to understand what this thing was for," he said finally, smiling. "It sent particularly piercing little circles of sunlight into the eyes of passersby. Zounds . . . the poor bastard even used it on me, just yesterday afternoon!"

"What a sad overgrown child!" Mr. Chadburn thought aloud.

"You have to be a bit daft, all the same," Mrs. Chisnutt concluded bitterly, "when you think that he preferred this four-pence doll to a real creature of the Good Lord, of good life and well-established reputation."

"The autopsy will enlighten us," Dr. Cooper finally decided.

It concluded with a verdict of natural death due to an embolism, and there was no longer a question of the problematic fright that kills.

Twelve honest and loyal citizens, assembled as a jury in one of the beautiful halls of the town hall, were in complete agreement on this and regaled with port and biscuits at the expense of the municipality.

The case of Gregory Cobwell was closed.

That same evening, Sigma Triggs and Ebenezer Doove sat down in front of two tall glasses of cold punch and lit their pipes.

"My turn to tell you a story," said Sigma; and he recounted in minute detail the account of the tragic events which had won him, for a few hours, the role of honorary constable.

"Think about it," he said, laughing, "that big simpleton Lammle thought he heard him cry out: Galantine! Funny, isn't it? Why not ham or sausage?"

Mr. Doove took his long pipe from his mouth and sketched cabalistic signs in the air.

"Cobwell studied architecture, he aspired to fame, he had some knowledge of . . . uh, mythology, quite extensive in fact."

"What does mythology—goodness, this word twists my tongue—have to do with this story?" asked Mr. Triggs.

"He didn't shout 'Galantine' but *Galatea*," said Mr. Doove.

"Galatea?" I don't know it . . ."

"It is the name of a statue to which the gods gave life."

"A statue that . . . came . . . to life . . ." whispered Mr. Triggs slowly; and he was no longer laughing.

"So I will now tell you a story, my dear Triggs," said the old scribe calmly.

He had some more punch and, with a flick of his fingernail, knocked the wreath of ashes from his pipe.

"In the times of the ancient gods, there lived, on the island of Cyprus, a young and talented sculptor named Pygmalion . . ."[12]

IV

Tea with the Pumkins Ladies

The haberdashery of the Pumkins ladies bore a sign that read: "To Queen Anne." A wooden panel surmounting the door bore the effigy of a woman whose coiffure was adorned with ringlets, who in no way resembled the images that the books have left of Anne Stuart, nor of the clever woman of Cleves.[1] A heraldist would have had great difficulty explaining the alerion[2] emblazoned on one corner of the painting, and the Pumkins ladies would have replied to the curious that, since this sign already existed when they had purchased the business from their predecessor, they could shine no light upon it.

The Pumkins ladies, splendidly primped out in saffron and sternly clad in surah caparisoned with jet black, were of good repute and considered wealthy. Their business was booming.

This Tuesday, the eldest of the ladies, the majestic Patricia, was matching colored silks for the embroidery of Mrs. Pilcarter, who would take her place at the tea table presently.

"Walker!" she called, "Walker . . . Where is that worthless girl, that she won't answer my calls right away?"

The maid, a pale young girl with forget-me-not eyes, was named Molly Snugg, but Miss Pumkins had decreed that hence-forth she would bear the name Walker, and that, as among the lords, she would be known by her surname.

Molly Snugg came along, dragging her slippered feet and wiping her hands.

"I forbade you, Walker," Miss Patricia said sternly, "from wearing that ridiculous hat with the bridle around the house when I gave you a lace bonnet."

"Gave? You withheld it from my wages, when I could have done without it," Molly retorted.

"Silence!" cried the wrathful lady, "I allow no back talk. You know that today is Tuesday."

"It's on the kitchen calendar," Molly said.

"Since you are so wise in this regard, you must know that some of our friends' wives will be coming for tea."

"What shall we serve them?" Molly asked sullenly.

"You will serve Savoy biscuits at the rate of three per person, a pound of Dutch Dinant cakes with honey and spices, thinly sliced, a pot of jam with apricots, and a cup of orange marmalade with candied sugar. You will place the decanter of cherry brandy and the bottle of mint cordial on the table. Later these ladies will sup, along with the worthy Mr. Doove, who will be joining us.

"There's a cold leg of lamb, a salad of herring and roe with mustard, Scotch cheese, and rolls," Molly recited.

Miss Patricia was thoughtful for a moment.

"Wait a minute, Walker! You will go to Revinus's shop and purchase a pigeon pie."

"Really?" asked the servant.

"Really, my girl! And drop this sardonic air that hardly befits a person of your station. You will set one more place. We have invited the Honorable Sidney Terence Triggs."

"Heavens!" cried the scullion, "the London detective!"

"Do not forget, Walker, to set the red velour armchair to the left of the fireplace, for Lady Florence Honnybingle."

"I shan't forget that," Molly said.

It belonged to the sacred tradition of the house on days when guests were welcomed. A comfortable velour-upholstered Utrecht chair sat near the andirons, regardless of whether a fire was lit in the forged copper hearth, but it sat eternally empty.

Molly Snugg had never seen Lady Honnybingle, but people who came to tea at the home of the Pumkins ladies could talk of nothing but her.

The maid who had come from Kingston three years ago had not failed to inquire about this person of high quality.

Apothecary Pycroft said, smiling mysteriously, that this noble lady sometimes honored him with her patronage, but could not or would not say where she resided.

Freemantle, the butcher, a rude man, only growled:

"Ah yes, old Honnybingle! Leave me alone, it's none of my business. Ask your mistresses, they know more than I do."

But the jovial Revinus laughed harshly in her face.

"I've never sold her even a biscuit, my dear. But if you're interested, in my youth, in the merry quarter of Wapping, there was a Honnybingle, who was no Lady, just a hawker of mussels and pickled salmon. She must be the same, unless she's one of her sisters, of which she had seven."

The painter Slumbot had ironically offered to sell her a portrait of the Lady, which he had painted himself.

Molly was thinking of pursuing her investigation among the city hall employees when Miss Patricia caught wind of her curiosity.

There followed an interview so stormy and heavy with threats of dismissal that the servant swore never to breathe a word about the invisible Lady, except for the necessities of the services assigned her.

However, she got an idea. In the immense Broody Park stood, at the edge of a larch wood, a singular building, a sort of folly raised only to the height of one story, with windows hung with garnet velour.

Molly had once ventured into the area with a delivery boy who was not from the area.

A game warden suddenly appeared and chased them ignominiously from the forbidden land; but, since that time, the young girl had acquired the conviction that the forest house served as a refuge for the mysterious Lady Honnybingle.

"Go," ordered Miss Pumkins, "and tell my sisters to leave off what they're doing and wash up."

Deborah and Ruth Pumkins were busy in the back of the shop counting spools of thread, bending sheets of pins, and making skeins of yarn and balls of shoelaces.

Molly did not like Deborah, who was sly and vindictive, but felt drawn to Ruth, the youngest of the Pumkins, who, but for the old-fashioned getup imposed on her by her sisters, might have passed for pretty.

As the youngest was slipping up the stairs to her bedroom, Molly took Ruth aside and whispered in her ear:

"You know, Miss Ruth, the detective from London will be supping here tonight!"

"Will he come?" Ruth doubted, pouting. "These policemen don't seem very outgoing."

"I've seen him," replied Molly Snugg. "He looks sweet and very good to me, and I like him better than Sergeant Lammle, who always seems ready to handcuff you."

"Perhaps he will tell us something about poor Mr. Cobwell," said Ruth Pumkins sadly.

"Something?"

"Yes, something only he knows: these people from the London police are full of mysteries."

"Then I'll ask him . . ." Molly began.

"About what, my girl?"

"Oh, nothing, Miss Ruth!" the servant hastened to reply. Her pale cheeks had taken on a faint hue.

She was thinking of Lady Honnybingle, but dared not say anything, even to Ruth.

A few minutes before the drawing-room clock struck four, Miss Patricia took her place in the reception room.

It was a high-ceilinged room, completely covered in canary yellow paper, furnished with canvas chairs, a polished mahogany table, and the red velour armchair.

A large mirror, of slightly viridine water, overlooked the veined marble of the fireplace and was flanked by two tall globe lamps, which were lit at nightfall.

On the walls hung daguerreotypes and two large oil portraits of gentlemen in wigs and frills, whom the Pumkins ladies had adopted as ancestors, though they had purchased them from a thrift store in James Market.

The central mantel clock, representing a bearded old man brandishing a threatening scythe, was mute, and a Black Forest cuckoo clock had the task of counting off the seconds with its sonorous ticking.

As this noisy mechanism announced, with a metallic rattle, the approaching appearance of the wooden bird which would launch its sylvan call four times, Miss Patricia, putting her face to the window, cried:

"Mrs. Pilcarter's closing her shop and going to cross the square! Come down, Deborah and Ruth!"

A few minutes after the cuckoo's cry, the assembly was complete, consisting, besides the Pumkins ladies, of Mrs. Pilcarter; a shabby old maid living in a back alley, Miss Ellen Hasslop; the stately widow of a pavement inspector, Mrs. Bubsey; and a bustling little lady named Miss Betsy Sawyer, who wore only a little makeup.

"My dears," simpered Miss Patricia, sweeping their faces with a smile, "shall we not wait for Lady Honnybingle to come? We know she is not very punctual."

By mutual agreement, these ladies agreed to wait for the invisible Lady Florence until half past the hour.

Could such a great, complete peace, such a prodigious stoppage in time, ever have been disturbed by other concerns, arising from a sphere foreign to peaceful Ingersham? What prophet of doom would have dared to predict the great fear about to fall upon them, and of which the end of Mr. Cobwell was the tragic prelude?

But, as always, it is best not to get ahead of ourselves.

The cuckoo clock announced the half hour, and Molly Snugg came in, carrying the boiling tea.

The Pumkins ladies ate little; Mrs. Pilcarter asked for a glass of cherry brandy after the second cup of tea; Miss Ellen nibbled her biscuits apologetically; Miss Sawyer savored everything with the expression of a greedy pussycat, claiming that she had such a bird's appetite even as she ended up breaking the record, despite the barely concealed gluttony of the opulent widow Bubsey.

Curiously enough, they spoke very little . . . They were waiting for supper, and the worthy Mr. Doove, to loosen their tongues.

Once the table was cleared, while waiting for the evening feast, they played a game of lansquenet,[3] in which Miss Sawyer, who cheated, shamelessly swept up the dried filberts serving as stake money.

From the kitchen came the sound and smell of sliced, roasted potatoes, a greasy treat of which Mr. Doove was particularly fond.

It might be too much to say that tongues remained still, but the general conversation was limited to the minor events of the week, which were, in a jiffy, served, aimed, revised, criticized, and placed in their fair light, according to these ladies' spirit of justice.

They scarcely spoke of the late Mr. Cobwell except to pity him, to celebrate his virtues, to point out, while regretting them, some of his petty faults, to condemn without appeal the dismal Mrs. Chisnutt who shamelessly tarnished the memory of the deceased, and to finally proclaim, with a mysterious and yet knowing air, that Mr. Triggs of Scotland Yard might perhaps know the truth to the story. Which clearly meant that the ladies present were convinced that not all had been said regarding this sudden death. But they preferred to refrain from forming an opinion and to wait for the supper featuring Mr. Doove and . . . Mr. Triggs.

At seven o'clock, amidst the cuckoo's loud frenzy, Molly Snugg, who had come to the front doorstep on some vain pretext, burst into the living room, shouting:

"There's the both of them!"

This prompted a new homily from Miss Patricia on the insufficient education of housekeepers.

Mr. Doove made the introductions, and the ladies immediately had a good opinion of the one they called "his famous friend the detective."

Supper commenced. The meal was very good; Molly Snugg had certainly outdone herself and the pigeon pie from Revinus got top marks from everyone.

At dessert, while the liqueurs were served—there was rum and whiskey for the gentlemen—Miss Patricia urged, in the name of all the ladies present, that these gentlemen should light a cigar; she presented them, moreover, with some very honorable ones, in a varnished cedar box.

"Now," said Mrs. Bubsey, her face inflamed by alcohol, "now let the London detective have the floor."

It was tossed out so indelicately that Miss Patricia protested. She had invited the famous Mr. Triggs out of sympathy and admiration; his presence alone was enough to make this evening unforgettable; she had never thought of requiring his memory of police affairs as the price of admission!

Pinched smiles creased the eager faces around the table; what a dreadful disappointment if Mr. Triggs, taking the hostess at her word, would only open his lips to ask for more whiskey!

Fortunately, the worthy Mr. Doove saved the day; was he not the news broadcast at that pleasant Tuesday gathering? He had promised to give some particulars of dear Mr. Cobwell's tragic end, details he had learned from Mr. Chadburn himself, rather than from Mr. Triggs, whose professional secrecy he highly respected. Perhaps the detective would correct any mistakes he might make ... On the other hand, it would certainly be more interesting to receive the tragic story from the mouth of the most glorious witness to the drama's end ...

And to let the good Sigma Triggs sing for his supper. He had nothing to hide, however; everything he related was already public knowledge, except for a few minor details.

His dry and sober delivery was not likely to charm any audience; but the ladies were delighted with it, saying to themselves that he presented the facts with a neatness and clarity befitting a former member of the Metropolitan Police.

And yet Triggs felt, as he spoke, a vague remorse tormenting him. It was hard for him to pull a dead man out of his rest, to offer him as food to these vampires of scandalmongering.

He saw again, in the pretentious decor which enclosed all his dreams, the poor little man contorted by some mysterious terror.

While recounting more and more briefly the events of the dramatic morning, he saw reappear the petty apotheosis of false beauty from which the deceased had derived all his happiness, from the naiads of the deeply pitted plaster to the pretentious Buddhas draped in antique silk.

"So," said Mr. Doove, "we must admit that poor Cobwell was scared to death. The example is far from unique. Remember the case of Sir Angersoll, of Bouvery Road, my dear Triggs. That caused a great deal of ink to flow on Fleet Street, did it not?"

"No doubt, no doubt," agreed Sigma Triggs, who remembered absolutely nothing of it.

"Sir Angersoll was a good draughtsman and, if I am not mistaken, contributed to a few evening papers. One day, he took it into his head to make a drawing bearing the caption: *My Depiction of Jack the Ripper*.

"Ugh, how awful! The devil must have inspired Angersoll to produce such an abomination, and the artist immediately realized this, for he locked the work in a drawer, with the intention of destroying it the next day.

"At night he was awakened by the sound of a window opening.

"He turned on the light and, leaning against the glass, he saw the atrocious face of the monster he had just created, brooding over him with a tiger's burning gaze. He had time to call for help and lost consciousness."

"A hallucination!" snapped Mr. Triggs.

"It was not so, alas," retorted Mr. Doove softly. "Sir Angersoll's servants pursued the terrible intruder into the garden and killed him with two shots.

"Two constables and an inspector saw the body and transported it themselves to the nearby police station, from where it disappeared without anyone ever knowing how.

"A few hours later, Sir Angersoll passed away, and the coroner affirmed that he had died of fright."

THE CITY OF UNSPEAKABLE FEAR

63

"The Chisnutt woman," said Mrs. Bubsey, "—I apologize to these ladies and gentlemen for quoting the name of a person of such low status—tells whoever will listen that poor Mr. Cobwell had turned his dead eyes, filled with unspeakable terror, to the silly wax doll we all know."

"So she took her time over frightening him," quipped Miss Sawyer.

It was here that, quite innocently, Sigma Triggs put his foot in it, as they say. He did it without malice, and if he hadn't exceeded his legal limit that evening, he certainly wouldn't have done it at all.

"Mr. Chadburn, the mayor, told me that this wax doll once featured in a fairground show as the terrible axe murderess, Pearcy. When I was still in office, I often took pleasure in leafing through the album of crimes and criminals, of which each police station has a copy. Well, I can assure you that the resemblance was, in my opinion, quite striking, especially in the image presented in profile."

"My God!" moaned Miss Ruth Pumkins, putting her hand to her heart. "What are we to believe then, Mr. Triggs?"

Ruth had very beautiful dark eyes and the perfect oval of her face was not made to displease men; so, from the beginning of the evening, Sigma had been regarding her with pleasure.

"Nothing, Miss Pumkins, less than nothing. There may also be coincidences at play. It happens, oh, how many times!

"Hold on . . ."

He collected himself, then smiled, sure he was about to say something that would interest his audience and especially his hostesses.

"I have often wondered, since my arrival at Ingersham, why your sign 'To Queen Anne' caught my eye. It was only then that I discovered the resemblance of this portrait to that of a lady of quality in London, whom the police took ten years to nab. Ruined by gambling, she had made a considerable fortune by looting, with remarkable skill, badly supervised jewelers."

"Good heavens!" cried Miss Patricia, and Miss Deborah nearly fainted.

"And what became of this abominable criminal?" asked Miss Sawyer.

Mr. Triggs shrugged his shoulders.

"You may not know, ladies," he said, "that the police are content to bring the culprits to justice, and then ignore their fate.

"It seems to me, however, that influences were put into action. The thief did not appear under her real name before the judges, as that very honorable name deserved to be spared. Psychiatrists expounded valuable theories on kleptomania on the witness stand. The lady got off with a relatively light sentence and then disappeared from circulation for good. They are not looking for her accomplices, although she must have had some, and some very clever ones . . ."

Mr. Triggs fell silent, happy to have produced his effect.

Miss Patricia declared, in a dying voice, that she would have the sign removed the very next day, which caused a general protest in which Mr. Triggs joined.

Why connect a purely accidental resemblance to tragedy?

They all took their leave at a late hour.

Miss Sawyer, fluffing her pretty tigrine dress, cooed "Good evening" to Mr. Triggs and expressed the hope of another encounter very soon.

Miss Ruth held out a rather feverish hand, which remained in his longer than perhaps it should have; but as she saw that Deborah was watching her surreptitiously, she pulled it back abruptly and turned away without a word.

"Triggs," said Mr. Doove, accompanying him through the silent main square, "you have made a real impression on those ladies, especially, I believe, on that good Miss Ruth Pumkins."

Triggs blessed the darkness that kept his mate from seeing the blush rising in his cheeks.

"Eh ... eh ..." he said; then he parted rather abruptly from the old man whose eyes were quite discerning despite the tinted glasses.

ᔤᕃ

The event which was to upset Ingersham a second time came a few days after the amicable gathering on Tuesday.

The Pumkins ladies disappeared!

One morning when she arose, Molly Snugg found the house turned upside down; drawers and cupboards empty of valuables; the safe open and retaining only useless papers; the best pieces of clothing missing.

Mr. Chadburn, after some hesitation since there was no evidence of criminal intervention, ended up ordering an investigation.

It came to nothing; the ladies had not hired a car, and no one at the neighboring stations recalled any travelers matching their descriptions.

As Miss Sawyer pointed out: "They were gone like sugar in tea!"

One thing made Mr. Triggs think: the sign of Queen Anne had been removed. But he could draw no inference from this bizarre absence.

He confided in Mr. Doove, who smoked two pipes before answering.

"It might be useful to question a certain Bill Blockson," he said suddenly. "By the way, please look at the calendar and check what time the moon rises."

"The moon . . . the moon . . . What has it got to do with anything?" exclaimed Mr. Triggs, completely dumbfounded.

"Oh, watch all the same," insisted Mr. Doove.

The moon rose very late, barely ascended above the horizon, and then set again, satisfied with its brief appearance.

"Very well," said Mr. Doove. "What would you say to a walk around midnight? The weather is fine."

At the appointed hour, Mr. Doove, accompanied by Mr. Triggs, took the path by the Greeny.

Despite the moon's absence, it was relatively bright, with a beautiful zodiacal light, and a vast dusting of stars battling against the shadows.

The two night owls turned the little bridge and, skirting the enormous Broody Park, walked across the fields, following the course of the little river.

"There's Blockson!" said Mr. Doove suddenly.

Mr. Triggs saw a small craft sprawled across the Greeny, then a figure tossing silvery things into the boat's hatch.

"The fishing is good," the old scribe softly chuckled, "and tomorrow a fair number of people in Ingersham will be eating carp and bream cheaply, because Bill Blockson may be a poacher but he's no thief."

He walked resolutely toward the boat and called the man by name.

"Damn!" growled a disgruntled voice.

"Police!" replied Doove. "Come over here, Bill. I don't want to get my legs wet."

"Is this a pinch?" Blockson asked without much emotion. "In that case, I'll pay the fine. Ah, blimey! . . . the detective from London. Quite an honor for three measly bream!"

"You won't have to pay a thing, Bill," said Mr. Doove. "On the contrary, you can drink a glass of good rum."

"Well, I wonder what's behind it," Blockson said, with marked suspicion. "Detectives are rarely so generous."

"That remains to be seen," replied Mr. Doove. "Come along, Bill; a short hour of conversation, perhaps less, a quarter pint of old rum, a good pipe, and you can go back to your fishing."

"OK, I'm coming!"

As they traveled the span that separated them from Mr. Triggs's house, the three men exchanged not a word.

Settled in a comfortable armchair, equipped with a pipe and a glass of rum, Blockson, who must have had a clear conscience, smiled.

"I suppose you want to put in a large order for fish," he said; "I spotted a nice pike, eight pounds at the very least . . . huh, what do you say?"

He was a big fellow with a happy face and laughing blue eyes.

"We can see about that afterward," said Mr. Doove; "in the meantime, tell us what Molly Snugg told you."

Blockson's face creased visibly.

"If this is to get that little girl in trouble, I won't have it," he grumbled. "Besides, she's done nothing, I swear!"

"And who said otherwise?" retorted Mr. Doove; "but I seem to have heard that you are going to be married soon."

"Truer words have never been spoken," the poacher affirmed proudly.

"A woman who is to tie her life forever to the man she loves has nothing to hide from him," the old man declared sentimentally.

Blockson nodded, drawing on his pipe.

"Well," said Mr. Doove, "we're listening, Bill."

"If you want to talk about the disappearance of those three shrews—sorry—I make an exception for Miss Ruth, who is a good soul—there's nothing to say, because Molly knows nothing about it."

"I'm willing to believe you," said Mr. Doove, "but Mr. Triggs here has come to know that she did not tell the inquest everything."

Blockson cast an unfriendly look at the great man from London.

"Ah! These detectives!" he growled. "They're not men, but devils."

Triggs was silent and smoking furiously; he understood none of this and, inwardly, he cursed his friend.

"Mr. Triggs," continued Mr. Doove, "wants to protect Molly Snugg."

Mr. Doove certainly was the devil, because he had just struck the right note.

A flash of joy shone in Bill Blockson's blue eyes.

"Really? Ah, that changes things, gentlemen. If Molly didn't say anything, it's because she was scared."

"Of whom?" asked Mr. Triggs briskly, speaking for the first time.

Blockson looked around fearfully and said in a low voice:

"Of her . . . Whom else would she have been afraid of . . . ? Lady Honnybingle!"

And Bill Blockson talked.

It sometimes happened that Molly Snugg couldn't sleep, and thought of her fiancé lying in wait in the dark solitude through which wound the Greeny.

The Pumkins ladies slept soundly; but sometimes Molly heard Ruth tossing and turning in her bed, as she also suffered from insomnia; yet the servant could not place the youngest of her mistresses into the same category as the others and was not afraid of her.

She quietly left her garret beneath the shingles, and as she knew which steps creaked and moaned, she managed to reach the street without making a sound.

A quarter of an hour later she rejoined Blockson and, settling down on the bank or in the boat, devoted a couple of hours to chatting about tender things and making plans for the future.

The other evening, she had cut short the beautiful nocturnal interlude because a light rain had started to fall.

She had run back to the "Queen Anne" and opened and closed the door with her customary caution.

In the dark hall, she stopped and listened.

From upstairs came the sonorous rhythm of Miss Patricia's breathing.

Molly heaved a sigh of satisfaction and slid like a snake to the stairs, whose massive shapes could be guessed at in the dark.

To do so, she had to walk past the door to the yellow living room.

This door was closed as always, but at this moment its panel was pricked by a small luminous spot, that of the keyhole.

The maid stiffened in an astonishment bordering on terror. But the curiosity of Eve's daughter overcame fear; she bent down and glued her eye to the opening.

Her field of vision was narrow and confined to the area illuminated by the opaline lunar glow from one of the globular glass lamps; it shone weakly, and its light fell on the armchair eternally neglected by Lady Florence Honnybingle.

Molly Snugg suddenly staggered, as if she had just been struck in the face.

The red velvet chair was no longer empty: a woman sat motionless there, her waxen face framed in heavy dark curls, her black bodice shimmering with jewels.

Molly did not remember having met her, but her heart sank as she saw the stranger's eyes fixed on the door with an expression of cold cruelty; the young girl would have sworn that this gaze of green light could pass through walls and doors and discover her presence.

She made her way to her room and triple-locked her door.

The next day she dared not say anything to her mistresses; but Ruth, seeing her worried, questioned her gently.

"It's nothing, Miss Pumkins,[4] nothing . . . I'm feeling a little nervous," Molly stammered. "Maybe the weather is getting stormy."

Ruth did not insist, but that evening she caught the servant with her head buried in her apron and sobbing heartbreakingly.

"Come now, Molly . . ." she whispered, stroking her hair.

And Molly, oppressed by her secret, panicked at the idea of another night full of mystery, confided in Ruth Pumkins.

"I saw Lady Honnybingle!"

Ruth's face froze like a stone.

"I saw her at the stroke of midnight, in her red armchair which is always waiting for her."

Ruth whispered, "Oh my God!" and left the maid.

A thunderstorm broke out that evening and continued into the night, which kept Molly Snugg from going to find her fiancé, and she locked herself early in her room, where she soon fell into a sleep stuffed with ugly dreams.

The next day, the Pumkins ladies were gone.

... Here Bill Blockson emptied his pipe and said:

"That's all Molly told me, and I swear she knows nothing more."

"Bill," asked Mr. Triggs, who had been expecting something quite different, "... ahem ... the appearance, ahem ... of that woman in the chair and the disappearance of those ladies ... ahem ... what do you think?"

Mr. Triggs had stammered, visibly uncomfortable, but Blockson didn't notice.

"If you ask my opinion," he said, "I'll tell you it's a ghost. I'm from the country and I know of no Lady Honnybingle either in Ingersham or for many leagues all round. By dint of talking about it and believing it, the Pumkins ladies have given birth to the ghost."

"Nonsense!" cried Mr. Triggs.

"No," said Mr. Doove gravely, "our friend Bill has just put forward a hypothesis which deserves to be defended before some Psychic or Paranormal Research Society; but, in the present case, I don't believe it. It will certainly be left to you, my dear Triggs, to meet a real ghost."

Increasingly displeased, Sigma growled:

"Nothing explains the bad things in life better than the intervention of the devil and ghosts, they are dishonest competition for the police.

"I would like to look elsewhere or to not look at all.

"If the Pumkins ladies fled from one of these creatures, they would have put less mystery and haste into it and left their stupid sign in place."

"Sir," said Bill Blockson, "that night there was a thunderstorm that broke oaks into sticks. The rain fell till dawn, and the front of the house of the Pumkins ladies was streaming like a waterfall, except the square left empty by the sign, which was still quite dry.

"Therefore, it must have been removed in the early hours of the day.

"It could not therefore have been taken by these ladies who, under pain of being seen, must have set sail in the middle of the night.

"But, of course, none of that matters . . ."

Taking leave of Bill Blockson, Mr. Triggs had the impression of shaking hands with a colleague who knew better than himself how to unravel the complicated game of imponderables.

V

The Terror on the Moor

"One does not say 'Mister' Napoleon!"

Such was the motto of Ingersham's mayor, who not only allowed his constituents to call him Chadburn for short but also scowled at them when they said otherwise.

He was a huge man, a few inches over six feet. His rock-hewn head was planted on broad, square shoulders, and under his heavy cloth suit of neat and refined cut rippled the muscles of a wrestler.

He made the law in the small city, the law of a potentate, which was nevertheless very good and satisfied everyone, because it was summed up in these few words: tranquility, calm, well-being, and wariness of troublemakers.

The strange death of Mr. Cobwell shocked him as a lack of regard for his person and his will; the disappearance of the Pumkins ladies aroused in him cold anger.

"Sergeant Richard Lammle!"

When Chadburn added his first name to his name and title, the Ingersham constable knew the storm was not far off.

"First, you will arrange to let the Chisnutt woman know that unless she installs a padlock on her viper's mouth, she will be obliged to leave the hovel which the municipality rents to her without ever claiming a penny; and that she is likely to no longer find a place to settle in the whole territory of Ingersham.

"Second, if the communal services office revises the terms of Mrs. Bubsey's pension, that talkative matron will learn that she is entitled to only a third of the sum allocated to her quarterly. I have no intention of proceeding with this revision, so long as certain remarks, deriving from that woman's imagination, do not carry on.

"Third, Miss Sawyer will have to learn, without delay or detour, that the proverb which I have always cherished above all else is and remains: 'Speech is silver and silence is golden.' She will understand because she lacks neither intelligence nor finesse.

"Bill Blockson and Miss Snugg's marriage license is ready and will be issued to them free of charge. There is a small unoccupied farm on the Peully, near a pond said to be full of fish; the Municipal Property Department has been instructed to prepare a nine-year lease in Blockson's name; rental price: three pounds a year, taxes included."

"Goodness," said the sergeant, "that's not very pricey."

"You said it, Sergeant Richard Lammle, it's not very pricey! By the way, give the Widow Pilcarter formal notice that I defer payment of the fine of sixteen pounds eight shillings, which she has incurred for the illicit sale of tobacco and spirits.

"Tell her I'm deferring it, but not canceling it."

"Well," said the sergeant to himself, "that's what's called putting on the muzzle!"

"Off you go, Lammle!"

The storm was subsiding.

The sergeant took a step toward the door but hesitated to cross the threshold.

"I must report to you, Mister Mayor," he said quickly, "that the ghost showed up yesterday at the town hall."

Oddly enough, Chadburn did not get angry; he sat back in his large leather armchair, removed a fine black cigar from its case, and lit it slowly.

"Where?" he asked softly.

"He was standing in front of Mr. Doove's glass desk."

"And Mr. Doove?"

"His lamp was on, and he had stopped working. He put down his pen and looked at the ghost."

"And then?"

"I withdrew, because I had to finish my regular evening rounds of inspection. The ghost passed me in front of the civil registry offices and crossed the inner courtyard. As always, he had his long beard, his loose clothes, and his bonnet; and as always, he seemed not to see me."

"Very well," accepted the mayor with a sigh. "I have instructed Mr. Doove to enter into communication with him. He did not succeed; this phantom appears to be supremely indifferent to everything. Bah! . . . it doesn't matter after all . . . Goodbye, Lammle."

Chadburn remained alone; but as soon as the door closed behind the constable, his countenance lost its original serenity, and wrinkles creased his broad forehead.

"Damn the ghost," he growled, "because there's worse than him."

He picked up a speaking tube capped with a whistle and made a call.

"Bring Mr. Doove! Wait, first bring me the documents I need to sign."

A few moments later, a young girl in horn-rimmed glasses entered and placed in front of him a wickerwork basket in which a thin bundle of files was stacked.

"Hello, Miss Chamsun. Well? And how is that outdoor cure treating you?"

The young girl blushed and grew embarrassed.

"We're moving back to town," she said after a long hesitation.

The mayor looked at her in astonishment.

"Yet we have placed such a pretty cottage at your disposal."

Miss Chamsun lowered her head, like a child caught in the act.

"It's my sister who doesn't want to stay any longer," she sighed, "and the servant's threatening to leave."

Chadburn suppressed a gesture of anger, then asked in a softened tone:

"Come, my child, tell me what's wrong."

The girl looked obviously desperate.

"I don't know," she sobbed. "People are scared. Don't ask me of what; none of us can say, Mr. Mayor. During the day, the Peully is a delightful place: flowers among the tall grass, fragrant rosehips, birds . . . oh! the birds, the rabbits that graze on sainfoin and barely run away when you approach. But come the evening, the night!"

"Evening, night," repeated Chadburn. "And then . . . ?"

Miss Chamsun wrung her thin pale hands.

"Oh, don't blame me if I can't say more! We're afraid and we don't know why. Are there terrible things that we don't see that one of these days could manifest themselves? You'll certainly deny it, Mayor, but I must admit that I believe it . . . without a shred of evidence until now."

"My child," Chadburn said with a kind smile, "when the nerves start playing tricks on poor humans, they don't go easy.

"Tell me one fact, one tangible thing, and I'm your man to fix it. In the meantime, I want to do something for you and yours. We are lucky to have with us a detective from Scotland Yard; he is said to be very capable, and I don't doubt it. It's admittedly difficult to launch him on a nonexistent track, to ask him to handcuff the invisible. But, just to reassure you, to restore your peace, I could ask him to look after your . . . case."

78   JEAN RAY

Miss Chamsun clasped her hands and tears of gratitude came to her eyes.

"Oh, Mr. Mayor, you are too kind!"

"One can never do enough, young lady, but don't thank me. I fear the Honorable Mr. Triggs will find it hard to put his hand to the collar of fear itself. Now then, let us not keep Mr. Doove waiting. I hear him coming."

Doove entered, carrying a large box which he placed in front of his boss.

"They are very good drawings," he said, "but I would not call them beautiful. Westminster Abbey is represented there without shadow or relief, all in lines. The correction is perfect but the artistry is absent."

"Well, well," replied Chadburn, "I ask no more of you. I like sharpness, correction, and completion in drawing. As for art itself, I have never taken a liking to it; I must overlook this deficiency."

Mr. Doove nodded silently and stood motionless, in the attitude of a servant waiting for his master's orders.

"And how's the ghost?" the mayor suddenly asked.

"He hasn't really changed," replied the old man calmly, "and never will, I think. He belongs to that dimension of space from which time is banished and where the immutable is to be found. He stopped last night in front of the big window of my office and I looked at him. He doesn't respond to my attentions."

"The archives remain silent on him?"

"At first, I thought not. Shortly before Cromwell's departure, a citizen of Ingersham, the Honorable James Jobbins, was incarcerated. He protested his innocence—I don't know what he was accused of—perished on the scaffold, and like many people who die in that way, swore to return to haunt the scenes of his misfortune.

"I believed that the late Jobbins kept his word, as has been seen before, but in the archives I found two portraits, very skillfully drawn, of the victim. He wore neither capuchin robe, nor bonnet, nor beard; he must have been a plump little fellow with a porcine face.

"It's not the ghost of James Jobbins that wanders through our town hall."

Chadburn nervously snapped off the tip of a pencil and muttered a curse at the specter.

"The history of Ingersham is, fortunately, very poor in crimes and criminals. But there was, a hundred years ago, on the steps of our town hall, an itinerant haberdasher named Joe Blacksmith who killed a halberdier who wished to block his way with a cudgel.

"Blacksmith fled to London and was never found. Does his remorseful soul, having not suffered the punishment of human justice, pay its debt by returning to the scene of his crime?"

"I have no idea and am asking you," chuckled Chadburn.

"Blacksmith was one-eyed and limped horribly. On top of that, he had red hair that earned him the name Red Joe. He hardly resembles our ghost."

"Enough!" ordered the mayor. "Let's leave this enigmatic character there until the day he wishes to confide in us at his pleasure. And as far as confiding goes, has Miss Chamsun done so with you?"

"She has," replied Mr. Doove.

"Do you have an opinion?"

The scribe gestured and shook his head.

"It is akin to the mysterious 'Them' of centuries past," he said.

Chadburn lost his temper.

"That's no explanation, Doove, and yet it's what I expect from you, or rather from your friend Triggs. We need him to take an interest in Miss Chamsun's case. Have him go and spend a day or two with her, in her cottage on the Peully. Our employee's sister is apparently a famous Cordon Bleu graduate, so as long as he can be led by the mouth, he will have no regrets."

Mr. Doove agreed to discuss the matter with Sigma Triggs.

၆ရ၂

One glorious Sunday, Mr. Triggs took up residence at the "Purple Beeches." The cottage took its name from a half a dozen of these beautiful trees, which cast a golden shadow over its garden.

Livina Chamsun and her sister Dorothy gave him a welcome worthy of a prince.

Even old Tilly Bunsby, the servant to these ladies, deigned to postpone turning over her apron for a few days, in honor of the London detective, who "was going to put all this in order."

Triggs wondered what he would put in order, but he was careful not to say as much, so flattering was the confidence of these good people.

Mr. Doove had been approached by the Chamsun sisters regarding his famous friend's tastes and preferences.

He hardly knew them, but he had enough imagination to find some for him. This led to Mr. Triggs sitting down at a table set with a pike with quenelles, a capon with stuffed boletes (Mr. Triggs was scared stiff of mushrooms), a beef pudding (this indigestible dish was ill suited to Mr. Triggs's stomach), and a cheese tart (Mr. Triggs hated them).

He made up for it during dessert with the lemon soufflé, the pineapple compote, and the French wine, which was of a good vintage.

After a siesta with excellent cigars, a gift of Mr. Chadburn, and made necessary by the scorching atmosphere, Mr. Triggs announced that he was going to conduct a little reconnaissance.

The Peully, an immense and picturesque fallow land, sparingly interspersed with overly arid pastures, appeared to him without mystery in the great sunlit fairyland. He walked thoughtlessly, decapitating the square stems of the figwort with a nervous cane, grimaced at the bitter taste of the water betony which grew along an anemic stream, and followed with a distracted eye the flight of a goshawk pursued by a swarm of angry sparrows.

"I wonder where They could be hiding," he grumbled, without his having any idea as to the identity of the "They" in question either. "No better than a flea on the hand," he concluded, satisfied with this vulgar image.

Shortly after, he realized that the Peully was not so innocent as it had first appeared to him: folds in the ground, sunken lanes, winding fifteen feet below the level of the moor, looked like traps.

From a gully rose a thin wisp of smoke, and Triggs wondered who, in this furious heat wave, had the courage to light a fire.

A quarter of an hour later he came upon a Bohemian camp, the dirtiest he had ever seen. It consisted of about fifteen gypsies, men, women, and children, grouped around two miserable caravans.

A stew that exhaled the odor of carrion was cooking quietly on a heath fire, watched by a hideous Carabosse.[1]

The leader of the troop, a tall ungainly fellow with the head of a bearded vulture, answered Sigma Triggs's questions with good grace.

They were in prohibited territory, for they were forbidden to stay in Surrey, but the border of Middlesex was less than a mile away, and if they camped there it was because they had found shade, and a little water.

Was he going to hassle them? They hoped not: they were so poor! They were chased off everywhere as accursed, although they did no harm to anyone and respected the well-being of others.

They had trained roaches, repugnant creatures, less docile than fleas, and expected some profit for displaying their prowess to passersby. If His Lordship would like to see, it would cost him nothing.

On a large sheet of cardboard, a boy released seven or eight shiny cockroaches, which began to run in a circle, somersault on a wisp of straw, and make startling about-faces.

Triggs noticed that the trainer used a long iron needle, heated by the flame of a candle, to force the insects to bend to his will. He didn't protest against this cruelty, for he felt a strong repulsion toward roaches; on the other hand, the misery of the gypsies did not leave him indifferent.

"You could go by Ingersham," he said, "and make a little on tickets there. I could ask the mayor to allow you a short stay."

The nomad scratched his chin in embarrassment.

"I . . . we'd rather go into Middlesex," he stammered.

"You are ten miles from the first town in that county, while Ingersham is but a step away," replied Triggs.

The other members of the troop had come closer and were following the conversation with worried faces; finally, one of the women dared to speak.

"We don't want to go to Ingersham!"

The chief nodded enthusiastically.

"Indeed, sir, we don't!"

"Really?" cried the detective. "Why not?"

"It's . . . a cursed city," the man stammered, "and the devil has a good hand in it."

"Come now," said Sigma, nonchalantly taking a fistful of change from his pocket, "explain yourself."

"Hey!" answered the man, "I believe I have said enough; the devil is the devil."

"We are poor as rats," the woman shouted over him in a high voice, "but that doesn't keep us from loving our children and not wanting to see them die of fear."

"We have stayed long enough on this unlucky Peully," growled the chief, "and by nightfall we won't be here anymore."

Triggs dropped a couple shillings into the man's empty hand, and gestured to him that he wished more explanation.

"Good sir," said the latter, "even for you it is not good to stay; an encounter with the Bull is always to be feared, once the sun has set."

"The Bull?"

"So, you're not from there," asked the nomad, "you don't know anything about it?"

Mr. Triggs confessed that he was not from there.

"Yet you know the mayor, the very stern Chadburn?"

"Well, of course!"

"Then," the man begged, "don't tell him we told you about it. He would get angry and find some way of making us miserable; he doesn't want anyone talking about the Great Fear of Ingersham."

"The Bull . . . the Great Fear," Triggs repeated.

"Fear is fear, and there's no explaining it," the nomad said gravely. "I suppose everyone feels it when the devil is on the march and approaches; but the Bull is a terrible phantom-beast, with the muzzle of a fire-breathing bull, horns as tall as saplings, and eyes . . . eyes . . ."

84   JEAN RAY

Like a mother duck, the gypsy had gathered her children around her; Mr. Triggs noticed that, despite their filth, they were lovely as cherubs.

"If they die of hunger, that is their fate," she said fiercely, "but that the monsters over there come to bleed them for me like rabbits, ah! God no!"

She brandished a hateful fist at the distant towers of city hall, burning like cones of fiery gold in the crazed light.

After an ample distribution of loose change to the kids, Mr. Triggs took the road back to the "Purple Beeches," wondering whether he had not discovered "something."

౪

After tea with sandwiches and sweet cakes which reconciled Mr. Triggs with his stomach, Miss Livina Chamsun offered her guest an hour of music in her "sanctuary."

Good Triggs silenced a fresh revolt of his being; as far as music was concerned, he only liked military marches, and he told himself with anguish that Miss Livina's sanctuary would not accord well with the smoke from his pipe.

Nonetheless, he found the strength to smile and say that he would be delighted.

The room devoted to the young woman's artistic retreats was a veranda with all its windows opening on a lawn from which one had a view of the moor.

An upright piano, faced by a revolving stool in green plush, cut one of the corners from which sprang a sort of stunted areca palm tree composed of fibers and sanitized leaves.

On the wooden console of a false fireplace, cinerary urns in glossy plaster served as basins for motionless fountains of asphodels and livid petals of annual honesty. The bottlebrush tapestry of the walls disappeared beneath a multitude of cheap treasures: a citole with broken strings, dried flowers fixed under glass with bassorin, fetishes from the Islands, framed German postcards, and marine shells.

On several bamboo tables ennobled with embroidered doilies, Mr. Triggs admired in turn a reliquary in gilded zinc, a stuffed rhesus monkey with a macabre profile mounted on a rockery, a marmorite vase with crumpled foliage, an Albin satyr playing the pipe . . .

"How do you like my little museum?" simpered Miss Livina.

The word struck Triggs, who suddenly pictured Cobwell's sinister gallery again; he could not refrain from remarking:

"You seem to me here, all of you, very fond of art and antiquities," he said. "Just like poor Mr. Cobwell . . ."

The girl's eyes misted behind her glasses.

"Poor thing, as you say, Mr. Triggs," she answered sadly. "We liked him; he always gave us preferential prices."

"He died in a very strange way," said the detective.

Miss Livina shivered.

"Oh yes! I wonder . . ."

She was silent and turned away, but her guest insisted.

"What, Miss Chamsun?"

"They say he died of fright. I wonder what could have been the object of this terror. He was a quiet, calm man who could not be denied a certain practicality, despite his immoderate love of old things; it's true that I shared this passion for antique beauty with him. But . . . I beg of you, Mr. Triggs, don't tell Mr. Chadburn what I just told you."

"You haven't told me anything, Miss Chamsun!" Sigma Triggs objected gently.

"That's true, and besides, knowing nothing, I have nothing to say; but the mayor is furious when we talk about it."

Chadburn clearly likes sealed lips when it comes to the tranquility of his town, thought Mr. Triggs.

"I'm going to play you something."

The piano sang melancholy things that pushed the guest to the edge of sleep; finally, Miss Livina struck a loud and final chord.

"It's getting dark," she said. "From where you are you can see the evening star at the tip of that Italian poplar. If I call this room my sanctuary, it's not so much for the pleasant things that I have piled up here or the few musical instruments that it contains, as for the evening magic it looks onto. From here, I see the first shadows devour the moor, the moon rise behind the sand dunes of Middlesex, the heaths change from gold to blue, and from blue to the velvet-black of the night. Shall I ring Tilly to bring a lamp, Mr. Triggs?"

The worthy man sensed all the trouble that an affirmative answer would cause him; so he declared that he would take great joy in fully enjoying the twilight.

"Ah, how happy you make me!" cried the young woman. "Soon, when the west is a scrap of pink watercolor, the nightjar will pass over the house. Tilly says he's bad luck, but I don't believe it; he looks like he's waving little bells of resonant wood. Do you know the 'Song of the Nightjar'?"

Mr. Triggs did not know it.

"I translated it from the German," murmured Miss Livina, "listen:

They call him the flying toad. Why?
He has velvet wings.
Borrowed from the canopy of the night itself.
They call him goat-head and say he is a thief.
He has only ever stolen the milky rays of the moon.
Maybe he robbed the sky
Stars that he rings in his throat
As the miser does with his gold coins . . .

"Ah, Mr. Triggs . . ."

Night had come; the detective was surprised to see the moor sink so abruptly into complete darkness, but he was greatly disturbed when he felt Miss Chamsun's hand on his.

It was sweaty and Triggs inhaled the sweet smell of her perspiration.

"Don't tell," whispered the girl, almost invisible in the shadows, "never tell Mr. Chadburn that I write poetry, that I recited it to you.

"He hates such things; he probably doesn't understand them.

"I respect him, and he's a very good man, but he's the enemy of anything that does not remain confined to the ordinary. Alas . . . He's a very down-to-earth man."

A yellow light slipped along the canopy and Tilly Bunsby appeared, a kerosene lamp in her hand.

"Don't sit in the dark," she grumbled, "it attracts unclean spirits. Tell me, Miss Livina, where is Miss Dorothy?"

Miss Chamsun uttered a faint cry of fright.

"What, Dorothy isn't home? She ventured onto the moor again. My God, great misfortune will come to her one of these days!"

"I don't know what danger she may encounter on the Peully," interjected Mr. Triggs, "unless she gets lost or falls into a bog."

"No danger!" exclaimed old Tilly. "I would like to see you out there, my good sir! It wouldn't be the first time that Miss Dorothy . . ."

"Hold your tongue, Tilly!" begged Miss Livina.

"Well, well, I'll hold it; no one listens to me here, anyway. Do as you like, my dears; but tomorrow I'm leaving this house and I'm ready to lose my good reputation if I ever set foot on this devil's moor again."

Suddenly, Livina extended a trembling hand toward the canopy.

"What is that . . . are those lights running over the moor?"

Tilly began to scream in fear.

"Men, horses . . . They're there . . . It's THEM!!!"

Triggs had rushed out onto the porch and was staring in astonishment at the strange sight.

Three resinous torches that cast long red flames were brandished at arm's length, and lit, with an eerie light, a group of ragged creatures, carrying bundles and sticks and surrounding two trailers, horribly creaking, drawn by whinnying nags.

"Don't be alarmed," cried the detective, "it's the Bohemians who were camped in the ravine, and who are going to Middlesex! I'm going to have a word with them."

The leader, who was walking at the head of the horde, recognized him.

"We're leaving," he cried, "there's something wicked here . . . Come with us, sir!"

"What is it?" inquired the detective.

"The children have seen the Bull!" one of the women shouted. "He wanted to take my little Greepy!"

"And then THEY arrived!" shouted another. "We feel them . . . THEY are there! We have to leave!"

"Sir," said the man with the vulture's head by way of farewell, "I warned you, because you proved to be good and generous. But I have nothing else to tell you. Come with us or stay if your life is worth nothing to you. We aren't stopping!"

They moved on, and Triggs, much more impressed than he wanted to admit, watched them disappear, the three torches playing like will-o'-the-wisps, until a low ridge hid them definitively.

"Dorothy . . . Oh, Dorothy!" sobbed Miss Livina, when he returned to her. "I'm afraid!"

Suddenly, a terrible cry rose in the night.

"That's her, it's Dorothy!" shouted Livina, throwing herself to her knees. "My God, protect her!"

Triggs looked around tearfully; he regretted not having a weapon with him; but among the ridiculous trinkets he saw a thick cane carved from medlar wood, adorned with a pink ribbon. He grabbed it, ripped off the silk decoration, and asked for a lantern.

Tilly handed him a small stable lamp, with a candle end in it.

"Don't move," the detective ordered the frightened women. "The cry came from close by, and in the opposite direction from the nomads. I'm going!"

He had not taken twenty steps on the moor when he seemed to be walking in the very heart of nothingness; his lamp was of little help to him, for its faint light was content to draw a circle of yellow light around his feet.

At that moment the gods stood by his side: the long distant dune of Middlesex lay fringed with pale gold: the moon was rising.

The moor was slowly stripped of its darkness, and Mr. Triggs was beginning to make out the triangles of dwarf conifers and the low clumps of viburnum, when a second cry of distress broke out, followed immediately by a terrible roar.

"The Bull!" murmured Mr. Triggs, his temples growing cold as if from the touch of an icy compress.

One of the moon's horns appeared on top of the dune, and Sigma saw the monster twenty paces away.

It stood out, bristling, improbable, in a terrible Chinese shadow against the lunar screen.

Triggs saw the formidable bovine muzzle, the horns stabbing the sky, the thick hanging skin tossed about in a furious swell; but he also saw two large human arms encircling a groaning form.

If, at that moment, he had had a revolver in his possession, it is quite possible that he would have missed the abominable target by ten paces, for he was a poor marksman; but he held in his hand the only weapon he wielded with any virtuosity: a club.

Mr. Triggs was adept at drills with a staff, which had earned him his only laurels at the mandatory police defensive gymnastics course.

Quickly calculating his distance, he rushed forward.

When the monster saw him, it was too late for it to attack. It took a defensive posture, lowered its horns, dropped its prey in the grass, and held out its dark fists.

A lightning blow to the flank, followed by a sharp blow from the staff's butt-end to the stomach and crowned by a terrible blow to the face, quickly overcame the resistance of the hideous adversary.

Groaning in pain, it tried to get away, but Mr. Triggs was not thinking of giving it the benefit of flight.

"Give yourself up!" he roared.

The beast made a clumsy little gallop in the direction of a grove of alders where it was no doubt hoping to find shelter.

Triggs caught up to the bull just as its muzzle, horns hanging down, capsized on a massive shoulder.

The cane whirled about twice and the monstrosity collapsed.

The triumphant moon rose over the dune, as if it wanted to take part in the detective's victory.

"Well now, you bandit!" shouted Triggs, "show me your ugly mug or I'll give you some more!"

He waved his club furiously, but the vanquished foe only moaned.

Sigma kicked aside a thick cowhide, still sticky.

"Good lord, I've seen that face somewhere before," he muttered, leaning over a big, puffy face flowing with blood.

"No, no, don't play dead, my good man. You have a skull as hard as the slaughtered ox you used to scare people! Stand up . . ."

"Don't hit me . . . anymore . . . give me . . ." moaned a voice.

"And you'll do well to mind me! Stand up, I say, and get a move on . . . nice and easy, otherwise I'll put a bullet in you."

"For . . . heaven's sake, don't shoot! I'm walking . . . Oh! Oh! you beat me! I just wanted to play a prank!"

Triggs cupped his hands and called:

"Over here, Miss Chamsun! Over here, Tilly Bunsby!" Soon two small lights appeared on the threshold of the "Purple Beeches."

"Miss Dorothy is here!"

But Miss Dorothy had already risen; she tried in vain to speak and showed her swollen throat.

"Oh! Oh! he wanted to strangle you!" said Mr. Triggs; "He'll get what he deserves, I promise you that."

Tilly Bunsby had the last word on the nocturnal adventure.

Overcoming her terror, she had approached the beaten fellow who was standing motionless, head bowed, at the orders of his conqueror.

"Freemantle!" she cried . . . "the butcher . . . Ah! the scoundrel, and to think that we're his customers."

Then came the sound of a slap.

⟨ᘛᘚ⟩

They were three in the mayor's huge office: Mr. Chadburn, Old Doctor Cooper, and Sigma Triggs; the mayor was speaking.

"I congratulate you, Mr. Triggs; though I expected no less from a former Scotland Yard inspector."

"Um . . ." said Mr. Triggs, embarrassed, "I don't . . . thank you, Mr. Chadburn."

"Just Chadburn," interjected the mayor; "but I did not call you here simply to sing your praises. Thanks to you, the terror of the Peully is no more. You set forth and quickly triumphed. Freemantle enjoyed playing sinister tricks on people . . ."

"Excuse me," interrupted Mr. Triggs softly. "Miss Dorothy Chamsun nearly lost her life; the strangulation marks on her neck are clear. Everything leads me to believe that the bandit operated in a more sinister way on the children of certain nomads passing through the Peully."

Mr. Chadburn gestured to brush these arguments aside.

"First, it is forbidden for those buggers to stay on the Peully and even to cross it; and there were never any formal complaints or even a reported crime. Oh! . . . I don't want to excuse that scoundrel Freemantle, but I care about the reputation of Ingersham and its citizens' peace of mind. If gossip starts, we'll see the venomous cloud of London reporters descend on the city. I hardly care to have that happen."

"It would be very difficult to prevent them," said Mr. Triggs.

"Not at all, Triggs. I will silence my people; they know me and know that I have a way of shutting up the chatterboxes."

"It seems to me very difficult to hush up such an affair," said Triggs. "For my part, I could not do it, since you yourself, Mr. Mayor, sent me to the scene as deputy constable."

"Who's telling you to cover up the affair?" exclaimed the mayor. "On the contrary, it will conclude in accordance with the law and the judicial standard. Dr. Cooper has just examined Freemantle; he concluded that the individual is absolutely unfit to stand trial. In one hour, he will be taken to an insane asylum, where he will be interned."

"Indeed," Dr. Cooper said briefly. "My opinion will be confirmed by a sworn alienist. Faced with such facts, all legal proceedings are closed, and the investigation itself should not be pursued."

It was all plain and clear, and Mr. Triggs bowed.

He hesitated a little when the mayor handed him a check.

"I don't know if I should accept," he muttered.

"These fees are due to you," concluded Mr. Chadburn. "I tell you again, you have put an end to a terror from which everyone here has suffered for too long. Mr. Triggs, you're an ace!"

Triggs left, confused, but pleased nonetheless.

That day he received a huge bouquet of roses and an album of poetry, the first page of which was devoted to the "Song of the Nightjar," bearing the dedication: "To my savior, the great Detective Triggs."

With this came a carefully tied box in which he found the citole, the strings of which had been replaced; a calling card stuck to the handle read: "May it sing your happiness and your glory."

Mr. Triggs sighed; he smelled the sour odor of Miss Livina Chamsun's moist hand, and he did not know why he suddenly thought of Ruth Pumkins, mysteriously missing.

That evening he treated his friend Doove lavishly, and in honor of the preceding victorious day, they drank French wine in place of their usual grog.

"This morning," said Triggs, refilling the glasses, "Mr. Chadburn told me that I had put an end to the terror of the Peully. Well! Doove, I don't believe it; that lamentable madman Freemantle couldn't be that Great Fear . . . at least not completely."

Mr. Doove smoked in silence and breathed not a word.

Then Mr. Triggs felt less pleased with himself than he would have liked.

VI

Mr. Doove Tells Some Stories

Mr. Triggs had become the great man of Ingersham.

Of course, there was no open discussion of Freemantle, nor of the mysterious horrors of La Peully; but, beneath the elms, where they whispered like wind in the leaves, they celebrated the merits of the man of Scotland Yard and told each other that he had greatly repaid his debt of gratitude to the late Mr. Broody, who had supported him, and did great honor to Ingersham, where he was born.

Hats and caps were raised as he passed, as if by a hurricane of enthusiasm, and it apparently took energetic intervention from Mr. Chadburn to spare him the noisy homage of moonlight serenades.

Invitations to dinner, to tea, to make the fourth at whist began to rain down, and Mrs. Snipgrass proudly emptied the mailbox, which was crowded daily with flattering letters.

He received a letter from a lady who did not sign her name, "since she was honorable," and who declared herself "completely disposed to give him her hand to become an ideal wife who would assist him with all her might in his mission of retribution."

The stranger began the promised collaboration without delay by denouncing the Snipgrasses, guilty of having stolen six lettuces from their master's garden to sell them "to that vile fence Slumbot."

To signal his acceptance, that same evening at eight o'clock, Mr. Triggs was to whistle, unless he preferred to sing it, the tune of:

For love
Of a braggadocio
Lady Skips lost her so-oul!

Mr. Triggs refrained from this musical declaration and learned shortly thereafter that the obscure beauty was none other than his neighbor Pilcarter.

A retired schoolteacher, Mr. Griddle, living on the outskirts of Ingersham in a dirty little house at the end of a sunless and joyless alley, invited him to a daily discussion of three hours length "on subjects profitable to unhappy humanity, eaten up with vices, overwhelmed with worries, and bowing under the burden of original sin."

Miss Sawyer reminded him of "the unforgettable hours spent on the edge of an impenetrable mystery which she would like to relive with him over a cup of tea or a nip of orange wine."

But the Chisnutt woman took the prize, begging him to unite their efforts—in a permissible and proper way, of course—to defeat the filthy doll that was not even completely wax and which pushed presumptuousness so far as daring to bear a Christian name: Suzan Summerlee.

Mr. Triggs politely declined the various proposals or left them unanswered; he only accepted, in the face of Mr. Doove's entreaties, the invitation of Mr. Pycroft, the apothecary.

He did so with pleasure. His memories of childhood were quite vague, for he had been sent from his early youth, at good Mr. Broody's expense, to distant boarding schools; but, during the only vacation he spent in Ingersham, he had frequented the drugstore, the proprietor of which at the time was a gentle and hospitable old fellow, whose successor Mr. Pycroft later became, after marrying his only daughter.

Of her, too, Mr. Triggs remembered something, the image of a pale, pretty little girl, with eyes of soft azure.

And, in the rustic setting of this village apothecary, Mr. Triggs achieved, through shapes and perfumes, an affecting return to his childhood.

He saw again the two high parallel counters of glossy oak, overloaded with flasks, jars, and pots of shiny earthenware; he reacquainted himself with the complicated world of hydrometers with long glass rods, mortars made of copper and coarse Irish sandstone, retorts and stork-necked matrasses, and distilling coils.

The sign was still in place, announcing to the customers the availability of decoctions of barley, couch grass, and licorice; cooked and carbonated lemonade; aqueous distillations including bread water, meltwater, chalybeate water, hemostatic water, and magnesium water; groats and tar, as well as white poppy syrup and capillary serums; agglutinating plasters; and Sydenham's laudanum.

In the lidded jars, Triggs recognized the carminative, laxative, purifying, and cauterizing grisailles of curly mint, wild thyme, carvi, and lacewort.

Bunches of medicinal herbs retained their places on the joists, releasing tiny clouds of dust with each gust of air.

Mr. Triggs inhaled this atmosphere and found it familiar, laden with sour, acrid, and sweet scents of lemon balm, iodine, vetiver, and valerian; from a carboy stripped of its wickerwork, three-quarters filled with matthiola water, that emanated a heady odor of red wallflowers, which seemed to the detective to be the very perfume of his youth.

Mr. Pycroft had been among the first inhabitants of Ingersham to welcome him, and Sigma had searched through Dickens's world, but had been unable to locate the apothecary there.

He had spoken of it to Mr. Doove, who had asked him if he had read *The Old Curiosity Shop*, and when he replied in the negative the old scribe had murmured:

"It's true that there's always time to make the acquaintance of one Mr. Quilp . . ."[1]

Later, much later, when he had finished reading that terribly sad book, he understood how loaded with pain and anguish his friend's words were.

Pycroft, short, crooked, stocky, despite his sardonic puppet head, was worth getting to know. He was a pleasant conversationalist and expounded knowledgeably on many subjects.

Ingersham trusted him, and the sick turned to him for advice more than to old Dr. Cooper.

He received his guests in a Dutch dining room, gleaming and pleasant like the wardroom of a yacht.

A line of Delft figurines ruled in procession along the paneling, heading toward a place of honor where a magnificent bust of Scaliger[2] was enthroned, haughty and solitary.

As soon as his guests arrived, Mr. Pycroft presented it to them like one of the Lares:

"He was the sworn enemy of Gerolamo Cardano,[3] a man of deep knowledge but a sorcerer, cabalist, necromancer, and doctor of the devil! I assure you that it protects me against the evil forces that are in the air."

So saying, his puppet face grimaced, but did not laugh.

"Mr. Triggs," declared the druggist, "honest La Fontaine's hare sat thinking, because he had nothing else to do, as you know. The small town resident spies on his neighbor, chats, recounts memories, and eats; he also has nothing else to do. More often than not, he chats in a pleasant manner and he eats well. We shall chat and eat well."

And so it was; excellent things were served on expensive plates.

"Try some skewered Greeny crawfish, Mr. Triggs. No, this succulent fowl is neither gosling nor pheasant, but peafowl. There's nothing better, provided you spare the truffles.

"I do miss that scoundrel Freemantle, for he had no equal in making a veal and ham paté, and I am convinced that the boor who takes over from him, in the hope of marrying the stupid Mrs. Freemantle, if she becomes a widow, will never match him. But that's no reason to do without this pâté, and I made it with my own hands. You like it? I'm delighted. These liqueurs ... heh, heh ... what if I told you that I make them myself, after the formulas of the excellent Raspail?"[4]

The evening was promising to be perfect, and there was only one shadow, which Mr. Triggs introduced without malice.

"I knew your wife," said the detective.

"Really?" murmured the apothecary, his lip quivering.

"She was seven or eight at the time, and I was not much older than her!"

"Poor Ingrid," said Mr. Pycroft after a silence. "She was pretty ... Her mother was Swedish, and it was from her that she got her Nordic charm. I was very fond of her, Mr. Triggs. Her health was never very good; she caught cold; the winters are terrible in Ingersham. She began to cough ... I can't help but shudder when I hear people cough. The specialists in London advised her to stay a while in Switzerland. She never returned, Mr. Triggs; she sleeps in a small cemetery in the Engadine,[5] under tall fir trees, brothers of the majestic conifers of Sweden ..."

Mr. Doove deftly diverted the subject of conversation: "I propose we drink to the success of our friend Triggs," he said. "I suppose the detectives of Scotland Yard would be right to envy him so rapid and complete a success as that which put an end to the terror of the Peully."

"Uh . . ." stammered the good Sigma, "really, I hardly deserve . . ."

"I once knew the famous Maple Repington in London," continued Mr. Doove. "Does that name mean anything to you, Mr. Triggs?"

"Certainly," lied Mr. Triggs.

"Do you like detective stories, gentlemen?" Both Triggs and Pycroft loved them.

"In those days," Mr. Doove began, "I belonged to a London literary club of some renown. Oh, don't look at me with big eyes: I was there as a copyist and nothing more.

"One day, Maple Repington entrusted me with a piece of work which I finished to his satisfaction, and it was no doubt for that reason that he related to me one of his adventures of which I was very fond.

"I will serve it to you as it was told to me. I therefore give the floor to the prestigious Repington."

〰

My parents intended me to be a teacher and it seems I was a diligent student. But when I had acquired my degrees and my diplomas, I found my intended career so crowded that I was forced to choose another path to earn my daily bread.

A bit of patronage from a prominent man of letters at that time, and the entreaties of some friends, allowed me to start in journalism, or rather in literature.

I will tell you immediately that I lacked style and even imagination, according to editors and assistant editors.

However, one of the latter, a very worthy man, was kind enough, with the sole intention of being nice and saving me a little money, to ask me for a novel.

The weekly for which he placed this marvelous order was called *Weekly Tales*, and it paid the good price of a penny a line, which to me was awe inspiring.

The choice of subject was left up to me, on the condition that it be captivating and have something in it to make the reader shiver like the kids in that German folktale.

I was more perplexed than I dared to say, and a week passed without my having the slightest inspiration.

I was then living in a cramped two-room apartment on an old street in Covent Garden. The adjoining rooms were occupied by an old, retired soldier, Major Wheel, a good-hearted man who felt it his duty to cheer everyone up.

He often invited me to smoke a pipe and drink a drop of his excellent whiskey, which was sent to him from the depths of Scotland.

Noticing my worried look, Wheel asked me the cause with his usual good-natured brusqueness.

I had no reason to make a mystery out of it, and I told him the story of the novel that "wouldn't come."

"It's not an ordinary thing," he said on reflection, "and I don't know anything about it. I have only ever read Walter Scott and Dickens, and one must not dream of imitating those men of genius; everything else is foolishness when it comes to books.

"However, I could point you in a direction . . . I dare not say it is a good one.

"What would you think of the story of a madman? For Colonel Crafton is mad, though he was, in his time, one of our finest cavalry officers.

THE CITY OF UNSPEAKABLE FEAR   103

"Do you want to go see him? He used to be fond of me, and we still exchange cards and wishes at New Year's.

"Crafton lives alone in Stoke Newington; pay him a visit on my behalf. Naturally, don't tell him that you've gone to see him to write a story at his character's expense. He would knock you out, that's for sure.

"Do you like Épinal prints?"

"A strange question, Major ... But my enthusiastic answer is that I adore them!"

"In that case, you're safe in Colonel Crafton's eyes, for he has the finest such collection to be found on this earth. He owns many of those children's images for which he has paid exorbitant prices, because he is wealthy and can afford such whims."

"Thank you ... But what is so special about your Colonel?"

Major Wheel sucked on the end of his pipe and looked embarrassed.

"It's hard to say for the man of common sense that I think myself to be. My former friend believes himself prey to the hostile actions of a ghost whose nature is unknown to me.

"Go see him and present my compliments; tell him you'd like to see his Épinal prints and, with his permission, spare them neither your praise nor your admiration. The rest will come of itself."

I was won over by the good Mr. Wheel's idea, and the next day I left for Stoke Newington. In those days it was still a village, with very fine grassy fields, thickets, and some fine old inns.

I lunched in one of them, under the sign of *The Merry Cartmen*.

Having finished my ham omelet and downed the last piece of cheese soufflé, I drained a large pitcher of frothy ale and asked the innkeeper to show me Colonel Crafton's house.

The brave man almost dropped the clay pipe he was taking great pleasure in smoking.

"Young man," he said gravely, "I hope you have not come to Stoke Newington to receive a barrage of verbal abuse?"

I must have made an unpleasant face, because he immediately added:

"That's what awaits you at the Colonel's if, by chance, he doesn't recognize your face, which seems to be the case for everyone who rings at his door."

"Is he mad or wicked?"

The innkeeper shook his head uncertainly.

"Neither, in my opinion. I even believe he is learned, and I know that he regularly gives rather large sums to the municipality, for the poor. But he wants nothing to do with people. Yet it was not always so."

"Tell me about him, will you?"

"I'd like nothing better, although I don't have much to tell. Ten years ago, he retired from the army to an old and beautiful house which was for sale on the outskirts of the village.

"He was not an affable man by nature, but he was far from the savage he has since become. He only went to the café twice a week, Monday and Thursday, and had chosen a tavern which had been slowly losing its customers, the Old Lantern, run by old Sanderson and his daughter Beryl.

"A year after the colonel's arrival in Stoke Newington, old Sanderson died and Beryl was left alone in the world, in possession of an inn without customers and facing rather heavy debts.

"Beryl was not pretty as such, but she was youthful and pleasant to look at; moreover, she was without fault in her manners.

"Crafton proposed marriage to her and was accepted without hesitation.

"For two years, the couple lived a life very withdrawn from the world, but perfectly happy, it was said.

"So the news broke like a thunderbolt, when Beryl ran away with a young student from London, who had come to spend his holidays in Stoke Newington.

"If Crafton was grieved, he did not show it; but he literally shut himself up at home, dismissing the only maid and managing the household on his own.

"In my opinion, marital grief clouded his mind to the point of turning this good man into a misanthrope of the first water.

"That, good sir, is what I can tell you about Colonel Crafton, and you will agree with me that it is only a commonplace story, however painful it may be for that lonely old man."

"Bah," I replied, "I have an excellent recommendation and I'll run the risk of a caning!"

The house of the former soldier was built on the edge of the communal meadow and completely isolated from all other dwellings.

Its facade, though old, was of solid architecture and very pleasing to the eye; the house seemed well kept.

It was scorching hot, and the air quavered as if from a baker's oven.

I pulled the lever and heard a tinny ringing at the end of an echoing corridor. It was not until my third try that the door opened with unexpected abruptness.

The inhabitant of the house was on the threshold, holding a rattan cane in his hand, and looking at me with a stern eye.

"Who are you and what do you want?" he growled hostilely. "You don't look like a peddler or a traveling salesman, and yet you ring the bell like those individuals who lack both education and propriety."

"I come on behalf of Major Wheel," I said, bowing.

There was nothing terrible about Colonel Crafton's appearance; he was rather small and plump, and only the blue eyes in his chubby, pink face were slightly ominous.

Hearing the name of Major Wheel, he seemed to become more human.

"Wheel is a gentleman," he said, "and would not bother me in vain. Please come in, Sir."

He led me, through a wide flagstone corridor, to a parlor, summarily furnished, but scrupulously clean.

"You will take some refreshment," he said in a commanding voice that must have been familiar to him, "but you'll forgive my not joining you: I hold to strict sobriety."

He went away for a few minutes and returned with a long, quality bottle of Rhine wine and an antique crystal goblet.

The wine was perfect and marvelously fresh; I complimented the Colonel.

He bowed and politely inquired the reason for my visit.

I immediately launched into an enthusiastic panegyric of the tender Épinal prints, telling him of the enormous interest I took in his collections, while confessing my surprise to see a son of Mars caring for such charming and delicate things.

His face, at first motionless and as if frozen, brightened a little.

"Épinal prints," he said in a saddened voice, "are all that remains of the dream of bygone men. They open another world to those who know how to understand them, although I dare not claim to be among these privileged people. Basically, I'm probably just a crazy old collector caught up in his own obsession."

An hour later, I was installed in the office of my new friend, before a collection of lovely images.

At that point, I forgot the purpose of my visit and could easily have sworn I was there only to admire those adorable and naive illuminations.

There were some very rare and, no doubt, expensive examples, such as the first subjects of Épinal in intaglio and colored with a brush; they stood alongside the grotesque figurines of Turnhout and the close-ups of Nuremberg. The adventures of Tom Thumb and Cinderella followed the more earthy exploits of that rascal Nietdeug, and the miraculous story of the sugarloaf.[6]

Evening was falling and I was thinking of taking my leave. Just as I was seeking an excuse which would allow me a speedy return, the weather decided to force my hand. As I rose, reluctantly abandoning a violently colored series of the misadventures of Mr. Distracted,[7] a tremendous thunderclap shook the place.

As I recall, one of the most memorable storms to have raged in half a century broke out then over the metropolis and its suburbs.

We saw, from the window, the leaves of the trees swaying like wild manes, while fantastic torrents poured down the sloping streets of the village.

Fortunately, the colonel's house was on a height, and it was this that spared him the flood that ravaged Stoke Newington and other suburbs of London that day.

Crafton watched the progress of the storm, shaking his head.

"I cannot let you leave," he said. "Unless you're a seal or a duck, you won't make it to Market Square alive. Anyway, communications with London must be interrupted at this hour.

"I can only offer you the hospitality of a solitary man, but I do so wholeheartedly; will you accept?"

I did so gratefully.

The colonel brought two beautiful globe lamps of pink porcelain, which he placed on the mantelpiece, and he closed the shutters, saying that he hated the intermittent flashes of lightning.

I leafed through the last picture albums, and then the colonel invited me to follow him into the dining room.

Outside, the storm went through stages of weakening and sudden upsurges; but the rain had turned into a cataract and roared tirelessly.

The room to which my host led me was most agreeable. It was a dining room with Flemish sideboards gleaming with the full gamut of multicolored crystals. A canvas by Gerritt Dou hung above the fireplace of black marble with white veins.[8]

To the desk lamps which the colonel had brought he added the soft light of a crystal chandelier, quivering with pendants, which made the atmosphere more friendly, despite there being only a fiercely solitary man and a stranger.

I thought that, for a single man, Crafton was well suited for running a household and even being an excellent housekeeper.

The cold supper, served on large but precious Delftware, consisted of large slices of smoked ham, a marinade of fish, a delicate *fromage de prairie*, and fruit sprinkled with sugar.

I was invited to help myself generously to ale and wine, while my host drank only spring water.

We no longer spoke of Épinal prints, but soon found ourselves immersed in tales of military pomp, which the colonel related to me with poorly disguised joy.

"You must understand, my friend"—he was already calling me his friend—"you must understand ... months of complete silence go by for me, apart from the strictly necessary words I exchange with people outside.

"Today, I'm indulging in an orgy of words ... It's verbal intemperance!"

He was smoking a big Bavarian pipe with smiling sylvan figures, and his eyes expressed blissful joy.

"Here," he said suddenly, "on this unique occasion, I want to break my strict rule of abstinence. What do you think of an arrack punch? I'll take a drop with you."

Rarely have I drunk a more consummate liquor than this arrack punch, skillfully spiced with lemon zest, nutmeg, and clove.

The storm had drifted southward, and for some time the rain had ceased its vain drumming on the shutters.

I looked at the massive Flemish clock and was surprised to see it mark such a late hour.

"Forty minutes after midnight," I said suddenly. "How time flies, Colonel!"

My words had a surprising result.

Crafton laid down his pipe tremblingly, cast a terrified glance at the yellowed dial, and moaned in a child's voice:

"Forty minutes after midnight! ... Forty minutes after midnight, you say?"

"Certainly," I replied. "As we chatted about such interesting things while drinking the finest liqueur on earth ..."

"That's what it is!" he shouted. "But, for God's sake, don't leave me ... Tell me, my friend, what time the clock marks."

He was white with fear and a trickle of saliva ran from his mouth.

"Come now, colonel, the minute hand is approaching the third quarter of the hour. So it will soon be forty-five minutes after midnight!"

Crafton let out a howl of genuine terror.

"How did I stay awake till this hour?" he roared. "Hell had a hand in it. What time is it?"

"But ... forty-five minutes after midnight, Colonel ... The quarter hour is striking!"

"Curses!" he cried hoarsely ... There she is!"

With a finger that trembled like a branch in a hurricane, he pointed to a corner padded with shadow, repeating:

"There she is! ... There she is! ..."

I saw nothing, but a strange discomfort oppressed my chest.

"The shadow ... The shadow of forty-five minutes after midnight ... Do you see her?"

I looked over to where he was pointing but saw nothing unusual there. I told him so.

He slowly lowered his head.

"No doubt," he murmured, "you cannot see her. She is so light, so subtle, the shadow of forty-five minutes after midnight. But you can hear her."

"A shadow that makes noise?"

"A specter that knocks ... that knocks horribly."

I listened and began to feel the first attacks of that irrational, abject, abominable fear which takes away all one's means of defense.

I indeed saw nothing, but I heard.

It was a series of distant, regular, very dull, horrible blows, a muffled pounding, carried out to a hellish rhythm.

I looked around with the gaze of a lost man, powerless to locate the place from which this noise rose between us, funereal and threatening.

One moment the blows were close and ringing in my ears like the peal of horribly cracked bells, then they drifted away and were no more than a rapidly retreating cavalcade, but the next moment they returned to the charge, stirring the air like the membranous wings of invisible bats.

"What is this noise?" I muttered in horror.

Colonel Crafton looked up at me with glazed, dying eyes.

"It's the shadow that knocks."

"But where?" I exclaimed in despair.

"We'll go and see," he said suddenly with a fair amount of assurance.

He grabbed one of the lamps and led me down the hall.

The blows were now less distinct, and their murmur seemed to grow airy, as if hesitant hands were now slapping them on the ceiling.

I pointed this out to my host, who raised his head to listen.

"No," he said fiercely. "The knocking comes from underground, in the cellar. Listen!"

He spoke the truth; a felt-wrapped mallet fell rhythmically into the darkness of the underground passage, the door of which the colonel had just opened.

"Come on," he said.

The blows grew more and more audible and, without knowing why, I dreaded approaching the place from which they came.

Suddenly, Crafton pushed open a lathwork door and I saw a spacious wine cellar, with many bottles lined up.

He lifted the lamp, which spun and traced a ring of black smoke upon the archway.

"She knocks! Oh, how she knocks!" he moaned.

"But who . . . who is she?"

"The shadow! Always the shadow of forty-five minutes after midnight. It is at this hour that she knocks, but I sleep and don't hear it, because I want to sleep and not hear it. Tonight you forced me to do so, you damned rascal!"

I looked at him: he was hideous.

His eyes were red and horrible flames flickered in them. His mouth gaped on atrocious yellow teeth with disproportionate canines. Was this the gentle and affable little man so fond of the delicate Épinal prints?

And, around him, the invisible gong-beater was now leading a veritable saraband of rapid blows.

"Dirty spy!" he bellowed, and his hand raised against me.

With unspeakable horror I saw that he clutched the handle of a formidable cleaver, sharp as a giant razor.

"Filth!" he yelled again.

He missed and the chopper shattered a row of bottles from which escaped a heady smell of port and rum.

But, as surprising as it may seem, I had regained my composure: I was no longer afraid of something invisible; I was now just faced with a lunatic.

"Colonel," I said calmly, "isn't one shadow of forty-five minutes after midnight enough for you?"

He remained motionless and let his cleaver drop gently to the ground, his eyes losing their murderous expression and growing lifeless.

The lamp fell and went out, fortunately without exploding.

I remained motionless for a few minutes, in the deep darkness; the silence was immense, and the knocking had completely stopped.

THE CITY OF UNSPEAKABLE FEAR

I struck a match and saw Colonel Crafton lying on the flag-stones, dead . . .

I left the house on the spot and, half wading, half wallowing, I reached The Merry Cartmen, whose innkeeper hastened to open the door for me.

The next day I accompanied the investigating magistrates to the solitary man's home, where the doctor found that Colonel Crafton had died following a ruptured aneurysm.

"Please have the basement floor dug up," I said to the police officer.

"To what end?"

"To find the corpse of Mrs. Crafton, murdered by her husband years ago in a fit of jealousy."

The corpse was found, its head split open by a huge cleaver.

I then told the singular and macabre story of the knocking in the night, and the doctor, who was no fool, nodded thoughtfully.

"I understand, as you yourself must have finally understood, Mr. Repington," he said. "What you heard was *the beating of the criminal's heart*, a beating tremendously amplified by terror, by the very hour of forty-five minutes after midnight, which must have been the hour of his crime. The case is extremely rare, but it is not without precedent in the annals of the Medical Academy. And it is this heart that broke last night after having pounded terribly. Heavens, how this man must have suffered!"

"However," said I, "that is not what made me think of Colonel Crafton's obscure guilt. I may astonish you, doctor, by telling you that that evening, throughout our nocturnal discussion, a vague apprehension had arisen within me."

"Instinctive, no doubt?"

"Deductive, rather . . . and it came from the Épinal prints to which I kept returning in my thoughts."

"Explain yourself," requested the doctor.

"Well, Doctor, I never saw a more complete, more utterly comprehensive collection of old pictorial tales than Colonel Crafton's; only one of the most famous stories was missing, a story that the smallest child would have asked for."

"And that was . . .?"

"Bluebeard! Crafton could not bear the accusatory image of the murderous husband, which was likely to remind him constantly of his own crime. And faced with this strange absence, my thoughts worked, you see, and, well before the haunted hour of forty-five minutes after midnight, I had begun to conclude . . ."

"And," added Maple Repington, "this dark adventure put an end to my literary career and opened to me that of the police."

$$\backsim\!\mho\!\curlyvee\!\wp\!\sim$$

"Good old Repington, I didn't know of that escapade," said Mr. Triggs, settling into the fiction and the venial sin of the lie.

Mr. Pycroft murmured: "So they drank arrack punch. I can make it for you, if you like."

"That story," continued Mr. Triggs, "reminds me of that of Dr. Crippen.[9] I saw him before the judge; he had a gentle, pensive face and you could tell he was a man of science."

"I'll make you the arrack punch," promised the apothecary.

"Ha ha!" exclaimed Mr. Doove, happy to have been able to squeeze in his story, "really, arrack punch? What we need are some Épinal prints."

"I like them very much," said Pycroft.

$$\backsim\!\mho\!\curlyvee\!\wp\!\sim$$

Mr. Triggs was debating with Mrs. Snipgrass the question of the menu he wished to offer Mr. Pycroft by way of return, and he was still hesitating over the type of freshwater fish and fowl, when Mr. Doove came in and announced the news.

Mr. Pycroft was dead; he must have taken a massive dose of potassium cyanide, because he smelled of bitter almonds, like an Italian marzipan.

"Mr. Chadburn has just appointed the jury," said Mr. Doove, "and he has asked me to inform you that you will be on it. You'll only have to serve on it for a few minutes, for there is no doubt as to it being suicide, and you'll receive an indemnity of six shillings fivepence."

"But what reason did that worthy man have for ending his life?" cried Mr. Triggs.

"Since when do we look for reasons for events in Ingersham?" asked Mr. Doove.

"And to think I was going to ask him for the recipe for his arrack punch," concluded Mr. Triggs sadly; "it's really bad luck."

VII

The Passion of Revinus

With the apothecary's tragic end becoming the talk of the town, Mr. Triggs's fame suffered an understandable eclipse.

He had no complaints; on the contrary: he had the vague sense that he hadn't really deserved it. The more he thought of the mystery of the Peully, the more he realized that the misdeeds and capture of the butcher Freemantle hadn't cleared it up.

Pycroft's suicide, for which he tried in vain to find a reason, had plunged him into a despondency which soon turned into deep melancholy.

He dreaded people asking endless questions about it and remained confined to his home, smoking endless pipes, leafing through the thick tomes of Dickens without managing to take any interest in them.

Several times a day, his eyes wandering over the sunbaked main square, he would murmur:

"Cobwell scared to death ... his neighbor Pycroft ending his life ... the Pumkins ladies missing ... Freemantle confined to an insane asylum. Good lord, only the baker Revinus and Mayor Chadburn remain before the houses opposite are to be completely overtaken by mystery.

The jovial Revinus didn't seem to care about this menacing state of affairs. He continued to stuff his shelves with immense pastries and large wicker baskets laden with golden delicacies.

Three or four times a day Mr. Triggs saw the mayor leave his comfortable abode, a servant in livery opening the door for him, cross the square, give a few absentminded tips of his hat, and step into the spacious atrium of the town hall.

The great Chadburn looked gloomy; the formidable reels of his cane must have underlined surly thoughts or challenged invisible adversaries ready to attack the beautiful tranquility of Ingersham.

Meanwhile, the weather changed suddenly.

The storm broke on a Wednesday, a market day.

The market took place without its usual animation; several haberdashers, dreading the Senegalese temperature, hadn't set up their stalls of boards and canvas.

A milk fever, weakening the cows, raged in the vicinity and a number of cattle dealers had refrained from appearing at the market. The afternoon, which was usually rather tumultuous—for at the stroke of three o'clock, the sellers of pigs and sheep arrived from Middlesex—offered little more.

Mrs. Snipgrass, serving tea and cake, announced to her master that pigs and sheep had joined in; they suffered from stagger worm, which made them unsuitable for sale and especially for consumption.

"Seems to me there's a lot of bad luck in Ingersham," concluded the good woman, "and now a storm's coming, and a nasty one at that."

Mr. Triggs looked at the blue sky and shook his head doubtfully.

"We have a good barometer at home," continued his housekeeper. "It came to us from Mr. Broody who apparently bought it in Italy. Snipgrass says the mercury literally plunged down its tube."

Again, Triggs nodded; he was thinking of the Stoke Newington storm in Mr. Doove's last story.

A little after four o'clock, people could be seen in the square standing with their noses in the air, and the tents of the Sheffield knife grinders and merchants, erected on the edge of the town hall, suddenly swelled like domes.

Sheep bleated sadly, and a ram, scurrying wildly, lashed out at an innocent Durham cow, which he probably blamed for the uncanny change in weather.

Six strokes rang from the tower of the town hall: the watchman was announcing the early closing of the market.

Mr. Triggs, a freshly filled pipe in his mouth, settled himself in front of his living-room window; however simple the change may have been, it was welcome.

If he had been able to pay more frequent visits to Cobwell's art gallery, now closed forever, he could have established some relationship between a fake *Storm* by Ruysdael, which adorned it, and the disturbing scenery of the moment.[1]

Clouds rose in turrets behind the houses, giving the main square over to an astonishing play of shadow and light.

Old-fashioned Paragon umbrellas moved in the distance, from lane to lane;[2] a white horse, harnessed to a timber cart, neighed at length.

Triggs saw old Tobias, the candlemaker, come out of his dispensary, bucket in hand, gesturing wildly.

Tobias was selling blessed tapers as protection against lightning and hail, and was calling out to customers.

Revinus was the first to respond, and the detective soon saw him returning home with a huge yellow tallow candle in his hand.

Large drops smacked the ground loudly, a few hailstones struck the panes, a gust roared.

At five o'clock the square was empty of people, all the doors closed and a few shutters already down, but the anticipated tempest still held off.

The harshly cast shadows melted into the general penumbra of an ugly slate hue. Triggs felt a strange sense of oppression slowly turn to dread; he rang for the Snipgrasses.

He got no answer: the bell was ringing in the downstairs pantry, and more than likely, his servants had retired to the outbuildings at the edge of the garden.

The half-light was turning to full darkness; the sky had taken on the funereal look of a solar eclipse; the tops of the houses were edged in lemon-yellow, and St. Elmo's fire appeared on the lightning conductors of the town hall.

Suddenly Mr. Triggs was convinced of an unnatural presence in his vicinity.

His gaze fell on the shiny black plate of the lock.

It was an ancient and solid mechanism, and it took a strong effort to operate its great swan's beak handle.

At that moment, however, it yielded gently to a pressure applied from outside.

"Who's there?"

Mr. Triggs was never quite sure whether he had cast this question into the wind of fear; he later assumed that his cry had been purely mental, imaginary, that it had only rung out within him, where only the echoes of dread answered.

Was he thinking at that moment of Bunny Smauker, whose ghost haunted his last nights in London? That, too, he could only assert later, without any actual reason.

The truth is that he was filled with fear and his means of defense had been utterly annihilated.

Yet when the door finally half-opened, he managed to make an effort. It took superhuman strength, like moving a terrible burden, but suddenly he found himself on his feet, his hand on the handle of his cane.

At the touch of this familiar weapon, he regained his spirits, which had already been slipping into the dreadful shadows of horror.

He didn't repeat his query, at least the one he had thought he had made, but swore, a curse clear and sharp as a gunshot, which restored his courage.

He threw himself against the half-open door and hurled it open, brandishing his cane.

At that same moment, a tremendous flash, accompanied by an infernal burst, dazzled him.

He stepped back, holding a hand to his eyes hurt by the searing light; but in that split second, he saw a long, livid hand clutching a thin, gleaming blade, surrounded by the bluish halo of lightning.

He instinctively threw his cane and heard a shrill scream.

The moments that followed were characterized by Triggs's indecision; the bursts of lightning and thunder were of such violence that the poor man remained petrified.

His eyes hurt; all hell was screaming in his ears. When at last he overcame his momentary weakness and rushed down the hall, he found it empty, filled only with the echoing sounds of the storm.

A furious current of air smacked him, and leaning over the banister of the stairs, he saw the corridor swept by a furious blast; hats, caps, and torn hangings all swirled in a maelstrom.

The street door was wide open.

"By Jove!" snarled Triggs . . . "in my own home . . . and in broad daylight!"

It was broad daylight, yet very dark, for when he reached the threshold, struggling against a frenzied hurricane, he couldn't see more than ten paces in front of him.

Yet it was enough for him to distinguish a swift, slender shadow fleeing before the storm.

"Oh no! Let it not be said that I let him slip away like that!"

Grabbing a cap that was flying in the air like a big dead leaf, he slapped it on his head and plunged through the turmoil in pursuit of the shadow.

Triggs soon realized that this was no easy task.

His bulk offered a large surface to the contrary thrust of the wind, while the slender stature of his mysterious aggressor gave it little hold.

The former policeman was visibly losing ground, as the silhouette grew vague and was already merging with the surrounding darkness.

"If the lightning wanted to do its bit," muttered Triggs, "I would forgive it for its complicity just now!"

The lightning must have heard him and agreed with his reasoning, because suddenly there was a flash. The figure stood against the facade of Revinus's bakery; Sigma saw a long dark raincoat, with a cap completely covering a small head.

"Hell!" he shouted. "A woman!"

Shadow had invaded the square again and it was darker than ever, but Triggs, though greatly struck by the unusual discovery, now felt certain of victory.

A dim light shone behind the glass door of the bakery, and Sigma recognized the flickering flame of the blessed candle.

The flame suddenly faded and then reappeared: the figure had passed in front of it.

"This time, I've got you!" yelped Triggs, rushing to the door.

It was unlocked and a frantic chime rang out.

"Hello!" shouted the detective.

He heard the sound of chairs moving in the back room, where the door opened, letting in a flood of light.

This brightness, shed by a strong lamp with an iridescent globe, lit up the squat form of Revinus who advanced, hesitating and astonished, toward his unexpected visitor.

"Well ... who the devil in this weather ..." began the bulky baker, "by my bonnet it's Mr. Triggs! It's an ill wind that brings you here today!"

But Sigma wasn't in a joking mood.

"There's a woman here, Revinus," he said. "Who is she?"

"A woman?"

It was a cry of genuine terror that the baker had just uttered.

Triggs moved toward him and tried to enter the back room, but the man resolutely barred his way.

"Triggs, you can't do that!"

"I order you to let me pass, in the name of the law!" thundered the detective.

Another cry arose, the cry of a frightened woman; a door slammed shut and Triggs heard a sound of someone's terrified flight.

"Revinus ... don't be party to a crime!" Sigma shouted, trying in vain to push the baker aside.

"A crime ... What crime?" stammered the fat man. "Are you crazy or drunk, Triggs?"

"Will you let me pass?"

"No," shouted Revinus, "you will not pass!"

Triggs could not entertain coming to blows with him, because the baker, built like an ox, was an adversary to contend with, and even if he could be defeated, the fight would take long enough to allow the mysterious woman to escape through one of the bakery's doors that opened into the alley.

Triggs thought that the unknown woman had already taken advantage of the time he had lost and that it would be impossible to find her again in this night of ink and pitch, when the storm had just burst into the full force of its rage.

"Revinus!" he said sternly, "tomorrow it will be daylight, and you will have to account for your actions."

"I have nothing to fear, neither from you nor the law," replied the baker calmly. "However, Mr. Triggs, let me tell you, I thought you were a gentleman!"

Strange words for a man he should accuse the next day of complicity in an attempted murder, Triggs thought as he walked home, bent under the gust, barely escaping the shrapnel of bricks and slates whistling past his ears.

ᘐᕟᘍ

Upon awakening, Triggs's first thought was not for Revinus or his mysterious accomplice, but once again of Mr. Doove's last story.

A torrential rain was pouring down on the city, filling space with the raging sound of waterfalls and rushing streams.

Mrs. Snipgrass, who brought him his morning tea in bed, came in practically without knocking.

"What a tragedy!" she announced.

"Eh? What?" grumbled Triggs, who was beginning to have had enough of this accumulated distress.

"The Scize dike broke last night over a length of more than a mile, Sir . . . The Greeny is overflowing. Oh, it's no longer an innocent moat, but a veritable river. If you want, you can see it out the garden window."

"Heavens!" Triggs whispered. "Just as in Doove's story."

He looked and shuddered.

There, where only the day before he had seen the green and tranquil vastness of the Peully, was now a stretch of gray and turbulent water.

"One man said that in the sunken lanes the water is at least fifteen feet deep," declared Mrs. Snipgrass.

Triggs breakfasted slowly; he laboriously collected his thoughts. What should he do?

He could argue no evidence against Revinus, and a magistrate's good judgment would hardly admit the story of the glimpsed hand and knife.

Sadly, he settled in front of the large window of his living room.

The market square, prey to the downpour and the gusts, was a sinister desert of water through which no one ventured; Revinus's bakery was closed and there was no sign of life there.

"Let's wait for the weather to clear up a bit," Mr. Triggs said to himself.

He was just giving himself some time, nothing more and, distressed, he knew it.

Around noon, things had not cleared up, and there was no reason to hope they would; on the contrary, the rain and wind grew more intense and again took on the appearance of a tempest.

Mrs. Snipgrass had just served lunch when the doorbell rang.

"Mercy! It would take a fish-man to dare venture out in such weather!" she exclaimed.

It was Bill Blockson; he was wearing a loose sou-wester, high rubber boots, and a sailor's oilskin.

"So, Bill!" said Triggs, happy to see a sympathetic face. "First, have a glass of rum."

But that face looked particularly serious.

"I'm guessing you came by boat?" asked the detective.

"Indeed, Mr. Triggs," replied the fisherman. "It's a disaster what's just taken place. There are square leagues of sunken land. Luckily, our farm's on a hill, otherwise we would be among the bream and eels by now."

He emptied the large glass of alcohol with visible pleasure.

"It's a tough job," he said. "I suppose the poor wretches wanted to get to the 'Purple Beeches' when the flood caught them by surprise. But I wonder why they took such a route in the devil's own weather, and in the middle of the night at that!"

"Who are you talking about?" cried Triggs,

"Haven't you seen Mr. Chadburn yet?" Blockson asked.

"No!"

"Ah, okay, I understand why you're unaware. Well, Mr. Triggs, I just brought the bodies of Miss Dorothy Chamsun and the baker Revinus back to town. They were hanging from the willows of the sunken lane that leads to the 'Purple Beeches.'"

"Damnation!" shouted Triggs.

"You've said it, Sir . . ." murmured the fisherman sadly. "Yes, it will give rise to yet another scandal, if Mr. Chadburn does not set it right."

"Scandal? . . ."

"Probably. It was already getting a bit of talk, but I'm not the one who would have fed any gossip. She was a young unmarried lady and Revinus a widower . . . I saw nothing wrong with that."

"And so?"

"Good Lord, people like me who spend a lot of time outside, at night and in bad weather, see a lot of things, but they don't think it necessary to gossip about them."

"So Revinus and Miss Dorothy . . ."

"For nearly three years, they'd been seeing each other in secret. In the evening, she often went to his house and when there was no one at the 'Purple Beeches,' as was the case yesterday, he went there.

"Ah!" continued Bill Blockson, taking more rum and agreeing to refill his pipe, "I understand people in love. If it had been my Molly, I would have ventured through a storm like yesterday's to see her and kiss her! But I repeat, if Mr. Chadburn doesn't beat his fists on the table, there will be quite a fuss in this damned village of Ingersham!"

There was a lull in the conversation . . .

Bill Blockson stared morosely at the damp grayness of the market square; Mr. Triggs was smoking furiously, and his pipe, as if powered by a bellows, scalded his fingers.

"Bill?"

"Inspector?"

To hell with this title to which he had no right! Triggs felt the shame of defeat deviously overwhelm him.

"The terror of the Peully . . . They say I put an end to it by exposing that wretched Freemantle . . . Is that your opinion?"

The fisherman's blue eyes rested solemnly on the former policeman, and Sigma felt comforted to discover a calm sincerity in them.

"No, sir, I don't think so."

"So," murmured Triggs, "the terror . . ."

"One moment, sir. Do you separate the terror of the Peully from the great terror of Ingersham?"

"Good Lord," cried Triggs, "does it really exist?"

"It exists," Blockson declared adamantly, "it's . . . forgive the term which isn't mine, but which I've sometimes heard Mr. Doove use . . . it's complex. But, for my part, I could give it a name. Let's be clear, though, because this name can only apply in part. Lord knows, I don't express myself very well and am probably not making myself clear."

"No," urged Triggs, "that name—that name, Bill Blockson."

"Lady Florence Honnybingle!"

"What?" cried Sigma. "But if I'm not mistaken, and given what you yourself gave me to understand, Bill, that was just a myth . . . some sort of imaginary creature."

"No," repeated Bill.

Triggs held pleading hands out to him.

"Look, Bill, if you know something . . ."

Blockson shook his head.

"No . . . I promised Molly I wouldn't bother with it, but I'm not saying the day won't come when I can put your finger on something that still seems to be only smoke."

He left after a firm handshake, leaving Triggs pensive and more distraught than he himself dared to admit.

౸

And it was on the evening of that dreadful day that he found himself facing this fear rising to the surface from the abyss of the ages.

The rain had eased; it had grown monotonous in the way it fell, not making much noise, but nevertheless a considerable downpour; in the sky the slate-colored clouds drove heavily by.

The buildings opposite melted into a wall of darkness; only on the floor of the mayor's house did a few windows take on a comforting pink hue.

Snipgrass came to light the lamps; his wife followed on his heels.

"Sir," he said embarrassed, "my wife and I would like to take the liberty of asking you if we could... could..."

"Stay with you," finished Mrs. Snipgrass in an anguished voice. "Oh, we won't disturb you, Sir, we'll be quiet and stay out of the way."

"Well," answered Triggs, "I'd like nothing better. Yet..."

"We wouldn't like to be alone at our place, in the cottage at the end of the garden," explained old Snipgrass, casting a pleading look at his employer; "on nights like this, people come together. Without the unfortunate matter you know about, sir, odds are that Mrs. Pilcarter would have asked you for a few hours of hospitality."

"But why?" Sigma insisted. "I grant you, it's not an inviting evening, as it's dark and cold, but that doesn't explain this need for being together."

"We're scared," Mrs. Snipgrass said simply. "Look, sir, there's old Tobias running out of his shop, a bundle of candles under his arm; he's heading for the cabaret, which he never does. Oh, they're coming out of the lane: Mr. Griddle, Miss Masslop! There's fat Bubsey and the whole Tinney family!"

Bewildered and not knowing what to think, Mr. Triggs watched everyone crossing the square diagonally, heading for a modest-looking tavern whose windows were gleaming in a welcoming manner.

"They're going to The Silver Mitre, where there's a phonograph!" said Snipgrass.

"They're running! My god, even that fat lump Bubsey!" stammered Triggs. "What sudden madness has overcome these people?"

He saw a little old woman, in a Greenaway hat, hobble along in the rain in the same direction.

"Miss Tistle, of the Salvation Army," explained the servant; "with her, at least, it isn't fear driving her out of her house. The dear soul's going to beg the people getting together at the cabaret not to drink strong drinks and to stick to tea and lemonade."

"Perhaps 'They' will come tonight . . ." muttered Mrs. Snipgrass.

"They!" Triggs shouted. "Okay, can you tell me who 'They' are?"

"We have no idea," said the servant in a low voice. "We've never seen them, but our parents talked about them, as did our grandparents, and they were scared, horribly scared, sir."

"Just because you can't see Them doesn't mean they don't exist," sobbed his wife.

"Ghosts?" Triggs asked with a shudder.

He received no response. Snipgrass slid the heavy gold-tasseled velvet hangings across their rods; Triggs had one last glimpse of the square, now empty, and suddenly it seemed to him that it had a huge, haggard face, livid and twisted with dread.

He sighed with relief when the last fold of curtain finally hid it from him.

ᗧᖇ

"The doorbell!"

The Snipgrasses, who had been keeping motionless and silent in their low chairs by the fireplace, rose to their feet with a cry.

It had been pulled with force and filled the house with the shrill complaint of battered sheet metal.

"Sir!" lamented the old woman, "don't make us open it! I swear there is no one behind the door. No one . . . unless it be the frightening things running through the night in the rain. No, no, don't go!"

"You mustn't!" stammered her husband, as the bell rang even louder.

"Stay if you like!" Triggs growled. "I'm going to take a look!"

He seized one of the lamps and, raising it above his head like a torch, charged into the darkness of the corridor.

"God protect him!" wept the servant.

The bell rang a third time as he reached the door; furious blows immediately shook the doorframe.

"I'm coming!" Triggs shouted, thinking he could always throw his lamp at the head of a would-be assailant.

The rain spat in his face as he opened the door.

A tall figure stood in the doorway, dripping with water like the very spirit of the storm.

"Inspector Triggs! Finally!"

"Mr. Mayor!" cried Triggs, glad to see a flesh-and-blood man where he'd been afraid of seeing some misty and sinister apparition.

"Inspector Triggs," said Mr. Chadburn in a harsh voice, "I enjoin you to assist me. Please follow me to city hall where a terrible crime has been committed."

"A crime?" stuttered Sigma.

"Ebenezer Doove has just been murdered."

VIII

Into the Pentagram

Barely sixty yards separated Mr. Triggs's house from the city hall; the detective crossed them like a frightful calvary of shadow and ice.

"Ebenezer Doove has been murdered."

The words rang in his ears like a formidable death knell falling from the top of the towers drowned in the night and the rain.

Chadburn had taken his arm and was dragging him along; as he reached the steps he grumbled:

"Goodness, don't tremble like that!"

For Triggs was indeed trembling, like a poor leaf in a storm; with an uncertain hand, he fumbled in his pocket and felt a little reassured: just as he was about to set off, he had mechanically slipped the warclub, that present from dear Humphrey Basket, into the inside pocket of his coat.

At the end of a corridor where the wind moaned, a square of yellow light stood out in the stifling velvet darkness.

"It's there," Chadburn said, still dragging him along. "That's Doove's office; that's where I found him. He liked to work late, and I let him."

"How . . . how is he?" stammered Triggs.

"The skull split by a blow from a fire poker or something of the sort. He must have died on the spot."

They reached the end of the corridor and entered a large circular room, with high and narrow stained-glass windows; bloody faces and atrocious motifs of agony and suffering emerged from a colossal painting depicting a battle scene.

"There!" Chadburn insisted.

Triggs stood in front of the glass cage where a white porcelain flat-wick lamp burned.

It illuminated the slumped form of poor Doove, his slender and beautiful ivory hand stretched over a large sheet of vellum as if to protect it.

Triggs looked away from the hideously deep wound and instinctively admired the handwritten lines ... the last of Ebenezer Doove, his only friend in Ingersham.

Just as mechanically, he read and blushed.

"A bit ... bold, no?" chuckled the mayor. "Who would have thought that this poor rascal was secretly translating Aretino's sonnets?[1] Leave it, Inspector. What do you think of this horror?"

"Eh?" said Triggs, jumping as if he had been dragged out of a deep dream. "I think ... what do you expect me to think? Who could have committed such a heinous crime? Poor Doove! The police will need to be notified!"

"That's you, if I'm not mistaken!" barked Mr. Chadburn.

At that point, Triggs balked.

"No, I'm not ... at least I'm not anymore, and I'll tell you something else: I don't feel capable of carrying out an investigation of this kind. Let's go, we need to alert Scotland Yard, and that's all I have to say for now."

"Stop!" said Chadburn, taking him by the shoulder ... (Goodness! He's got a heavy and hard grip, the mayor of Ingersham does!) "Stop, Triggs! Let's imagine we're on an island for now, left to our own resources. In a sort of stupid aversion to modernism, which I now deplore, we have neither telephones nor any means of rapid transport here. A messenger sent through the night and the tempest would not arrive in London before dawn, and there would still be a question of finding such a messenger. And I want to get my hands on the abominable creature that committed this crime before daybreak, do you hear me?"

"And how will you do it?" cried Triggs.

"Strange question for a policeman," chuckled the mayor. "But it doesn't matter, there are two of us, because I need your help. What do you have to say about this?"

With his finger, the mayor pointed to long white lines traced on the flagstones that were catching the light of the lamp.

"Well..." murmured Triggs, "it seems to me... but yes, I know what that is, it's a pentagram!"

"The great weapon of wizards. Are you at all versed in the occult, Mr. Triggs?"

"Not in the slightest, but I happen to know this figure and its uses. It's used to, uh... drive away ghosts."

"Or to capture them perhaps ... I believe, Triggs, that good Mr. Doove had taken it into his head to play a dirty trick on the city hall ghost by setting this trap for him."

"The city hall ghost ..." repeated Mr. Triggs. "He told me about it at one point."

"Perhaps he added that nothing is more real than this damned ghost; I have my own idea on the matter. Laugh if you like, Triggs, but wait until dawn to do so. Tonight, I intend to act, and I will tell you without hesitation that, faced with the danger of this singular trap, the ghost took revenge."

"And killed Mr. Doove?"

"Why not? If I were a storyteller like Doove, I could give you examples!"

"What are you planning to do?" asked Triggs, exhausted in thought and strength.

"To be done with this ghost! If tomorrow your friends at Scotland Yard, whom we will be obliged to call for help, want to work in their own way, they will do so; but tonight, I'm taking charge of the case. Follow me to my office."

Triggs was defeated; he cast a last look full of dread and distress at the corpse of Mr. Doove and allowed himself to be led away by the mayor.

The burgomaster's cabinet he entered possessed the gloomy austerity of a courtroom. A seven-branched candelabrum with lighted tapers struggled without much advantage against the darkness.

The darkness belonged not only to the night, but to the atmosphere and to the things themselves: it flowed from the Carmelite hangings, the thick window curtains, the wainscoting of ugly sessile oak. It oozed out of the parquet floor with its wide crossed slats and from the checkerboard crests emblazoned on the walls. It sat curled up in the two enormous leather armchairs, lay on the enormous table, and spilled silently out of the huge mirror where the sevenfold reflection of the candles quivered.

"Triggs," said Mr. Chadburn, "go and triple-lock the door and slide the bolt. Then make a thorough inspection of this room. Establish that there's no secret passage—I give you my word that there are none, but that doesn't matter!—check to see that nobody is hiding behind the curtains, and examine the latches of the windows."

Sigma obeyed, without asking the reason for the order; it took him some time, and he was comforted by having something to do, which drove away his fever and calmed his spirits.

He even went so far, under the icy gaze of Mr. Chadburn, motionless in his chair, as to look under the table and move a silvery nickel alloy paperweight crushing a sheaf of blank sheets.

"An iron damper seals the chimney, to prevent drafts," explained the mayor. "There is no way out there either. Do you understand what I'm getting at?"

"Uh, yes . . . that is, more or less," Triggs muttered.

"No one can get in here, unless they pass through this big oak door, or the shuttered windows that are just as solid, or the walls which are considerably thick."

"No doubt!"

"And yet," continued the mayor, lowering his voice, "I'm expecting someone who laughs at such obstacles, and that someone is the assassin of Doove."

"The ghost!" cried Mr. Triggs in horror.

"Himself, Triggs," thundered Chadburn, "and I shall have him! Look at your feet!"

The detective saw white lines running across the floor and disappearing into the shadows.

"The magic pentagram!"

"You said it . . . and I hope to be luckier than the poor late Doove and imprison the villainous spirit there."

"Unless he knocks us out," replied Triggs mechanically.

"Unless he knocks us out," repeated Chadburn.

With a heavy sigh, Triggs sank into the other chair; for a moment, he thought that he was taking his place in the heart of a vast web of charlatanism which one day his former colleagues would laugh at, but this moment was brief and the atmosphere took him in its grip: he awaited the ghost.

"Nothing compels us to maintain a silent vigil, Triggs," Chadburn said. "I regret having neither port nor whiskey here; but light your pipe if you have it on you. And let's chat if you feel up to it."

Triggs found himself at a loss and only grunted a few words; then Chadburn spoke.

He spoke well but talked of things of little interest to the detective; dissertations on topics such as Roman design left him cold as ice; he missed the stories of his poor departed friend.

Chadburn sensed it and deftly took the discussion in another direction.

In the end, they talked about Doove.

"He told curious stories," said Triggs, "and knew how to bring them to life. But what I appreciated most about him was his beautiful handwriting . . . What writing, what calligraphy, Mr. Chadburn! Rarely do two such artists arise in one century. But he was modest . . . I believe that, if he had wanted to undertake engraving, he could have claimed fame, if not fortune. He refused to do so, although one day I did notice two small acid stains on his hand. 'Hey, you rascal, Doove,' I told him, 'I'll bet you're practicing engraving on the sly!'"

Triggs was off and running.

"There was one day I clearly offended him. Now I really regret it. I told him, 'Doove, if you had the strength of a tiger, instead of having in your superb hand only the strength it takes to snuff a candle, I'd send a note to my old boss Humph'Basket.'

"He looked at me, bewildered, and asked me to explain myself.

"I knew a chap—or rather, I only ever got to know his hand, because it almost wrung my neck like a pathetic chicken—who was the most skillful engraver who ever lived under the skies of the island: he drew the designs of banknotes beautifully, without being invited to do so by the Bank of England.

"Ha ha! Doove was pretty offended by the comparison and I had to apologize."

Mr. Chadburn deigned to laugh and admitted that Mr. Triggs's story was entertaining.

The candles were rapidly coming to the end of their existence; a flame dropping faster than the others made a candle ring sputter.

"Mr. Triggs," the mayor suggested, "if we don't want to end up in the dark, we'd better conserve our light: I neglected to bring along extra candles."

They left two of the tapers burning, and Triggs thought there was little difference between the complete darkness that the mayor of Ingersham had just apprehensively forecast and what light still lingered.

The walls had vanished into darkness; he could barely see the squat shape of Mr. Chadburn in his armchair and the mayor's unruly hair, on which played a ray of light.

On the floor, the white outline of the exorcising form was oddly crisp and clear.

"Assuming the spirit comes, if he can't get out of that satanic pentagram, we'll have made some progress . . . but you can't hang a ghost," said Mr. Triggs, who was recovering some sound reason.

Mr. Chadburn only grunted.

"And we would make fools of ourselves."

"If the good people of New Scotland Yard really want to hang everyone, maybe they can find them," chuckled the mayor. "In the meantime, I'm sticking to my plan."

Through the moaning wind, Triggs heard the distant chime of the belfry clock, but he neglected to count how many times it struck, attentive to certain facts that suddenly stood out in his mind.

"Mr. Chadburn?"

"Just Chadburn, Triggs."

"I don't like that," Sigma responded. "It sounds rude and uncivil to me, so I won't do it, whether you like it or not, sir.

"Just now you pointed out to me that the unfortunate Doove was translating a sonnet by Aretino. I don't know what that means. I hadn't heard that name until now, but you were talking about a translation; I'm quite surprised not to have seen the text which he must have been using to make it . . ."

"Really?" asked the mayor. "There was none there?"

"There was not," said the detective. "In what language did your Aretino write?"

"Well, in Italian!"

"In that case, it was indeed a translation, as you said, but the text to be translated was missing. And . . . That's not all."

"Go on, Triggs," encouraged the mayor.

"Doove was a first-rate calligrapher; I gladly humble myself before his memory by proclaiming that I don't come close to him in that noble art. I saw the quill that had fallen from his hand . . . Since when, Mr. Chadburn, does a calligrapher like the late Mr. Doove write on vellum with a nib other than a Woodstock?"

"Eh?" cried Chadburn. "I'm not following you."

"A professional would never have done otherwise, and I'll tell you something else, Mr. Mayor: the lines on the vellum were written with a Woodstock pen. I know it. And the ink used: well, Mr. Mayor, it was the kind we call 'fade-resistant ink'; it dries very slowly, and its color turns into a beautiful shiny black."

"I don't know what you're getting at, Triggs."

"This, Mr. Chadburn: Doove was writing something else when he was killed, with another pen, another ink, and not on vellum."

"So?"

"The assassin must have taken some interest in what he was writing, since he removed it and replaced it with a text at least five or six days old! These are not the games of ghosts . . . although I know nothing of the manners and habits of those rascals."

"Mr. Triggs," said the mayor of Ingersham slowly, "you are very modest in claiming that you are not, or are no longer, a detective."

Triggs fell silent; he had nothing more to say; he had spoken more as an expert in beautiful italic longhand than as policeman.

"That's all, Triggs?"

"That's all, Mayor."

After that, the silence was tremendous, to the point of being populated by a thousand nonexistent whispers.

Sigma's pipe went out; again, the tower clock jack struck the hour, and Triggs counted twelve strokes.

"Midnight!"

Mr. Chadburn said nothing, and his companion on watch repeated his "Midnight" without receiving an answer.

Then, just as Triggs thought he was still detecting the last vibrations of the final stroke of the hour, he felt a presence.

Someone was moving slowly in the darkness.

The candlewicks charred and the flames plunged halfway into the melted wax, growing more and more stingy with their light.

Yet Triggs no longer perceived just a velvety gliding, but saw a form advancing toward him, a shadow among shadows.

"Mr. Chadburn," he cried, "someone's just entered!"

The mayor neither moved nor spoke, but one of the candles suddenly shot out a tall, crackling flame.

Triggs saw a whiteness hanging six feet above him, a hideously grimacing face that seemed to float in the darkness.

He screamed ... A spectral hand sprang up, disappeared, swallowed by the darkness, reappeared and, suddenly, took him by the nape of his neck.

A hideous clarity passed across his eyes; he tried to call Chadburn for help, but a pear of anguish swelled in his throat as it was crushed by an iron fist.[2]

He gestured vainly in defense, tried to get up, spun on his heels, and fell.

The waxed floor was slippery; Triggs slid as if spewed from a fairground slide, but this ridiculous pirouette tore him free from the clutches of the invisible.

He found himself on his feet, waving his arms, yelling, and ran to the fireplace where he grabbed the candelabrum.

Four or five flames rose gently at the tip of the wicks, and a sheet of light flowed into the room.

Triggs, in a dreadful voice, cried out for help.

୧୨୯

Constable Richard Lammle hesitated before crossing the white line of the pentagram, then, overcoming a visible repulsion, he leaned over the corpse.

"Fractured skull," he whispered, "just like Mr. Doove . . . Lord, what a misfortune . . . our mayor, Mr. Chadburn!"

He turned away, tears streaming down his cheeks.

Triggs, motionless, frozen as a statue, without a thought in his head, gazed at the remains of the mayor, lying in the middle of the magical figure.

"How did it happen, Inspector? Oh, I should really ask 'What happened?'" moaned Lammle, turning his desperate eyes to Triggs.

Triggs sighed loudly and seemed to come out of a deep dream.

"I'll notify Scotland Yard," he said. "Find me someone who can get to London in the least amount of time."

It was Bill Blockson who delivered the letter.

It was addressed to Humphrey Basket at Station 2 in Rotherhite, but Triggs still didn't know that his former boss had just been appointed senior detective in the Yard's Criminal Investigations Squad.

IX

The 28 Days of Mr. Basket

"He is a devilishly solid man, in spite of his age; he almost kicked the bucket, Mr. Basket," said old Doctor Cooper. "But the danger has passed. Before it gets dark, the fever will break completely."

"Hmm, I have trouble seeing old Triggs making his exit from a measly fever," opined the inspector.

"And you're right to, but he was nearly strangled or rather had his cervical vertebrae ruptured like a common hanged man. Zounds, what a terrible grip that mysterious assassin must have had!"

Basket nodded with a grunt; for three days he had sat by the bedside of the delirious Triggs, who, in his fever, spoke of strange and frightful things.

A finger tapped softly on the door, and old Snipgrass poked her head through the opening.

"Bill Blockson is here; he's asking to see the gentleman from the London police."

Blockson introduced himself, twisting his cap between his fingers.

"I found her, sir . . ."

"Ah . . . very good, Blockson."

"She drowned in the sunken lane that leads to the Middlesex border. The flood must have surprised her there. She's been dead for a few days and isn't a pretty sight."

"Put her in the cellar of the city hall and use all the ice you can find; you have to set up a kind of icehouse, do you understand?"

Bill understood and left, promising to carry out his mission.

Old Cooper was a good prophet, for Triggs awoke around dusk and, in a voice still weak, declared that he was hungry.

When he recognized Humphrey Basket, his lips trembled.

"They've come from Scotland Yard?" he asked.

"*They* haven't come," replied his former chief, "only *me*; I've been with the Yard for a month now, Sigma."

Triggs closed his eyes.

"Good God, I'm so relieved! I'd never . . . Do you understand, Chief?"

"Certainly. Now, my dear old Triggs, you're going to have a bowl of broth, a bit of chicken, and get a little more rest."

"I want to talk right now."

"About the weather, if you like, Sigma-Tau, though when it comes to the weather, there's little to brag about in this damned town. Let's hold off on the serious matters till tomorrow."

But when Triggs had restored himself, he insisted so much that Basket had to give in.

"You've always had a wonderful memory, Triggs; I hope it will help you, because we'll need it."

"I won't leave out a single detail . . . not one, do you hear me, Chief?"

Triggs spoke until the hour grew late, and Basket finally put an end to his flow of words.

"We'll pick it up tomorrow, like in the serials," he ordered.

And again, the day was fading when Triggs, tired but visibly relieved, stopped talking.

"I've told you everything, Chief."

"Very well, Sigma-Tau; now it's my turn to tell you something. When I mentioned Ingersham to my bosses, they gave me carte blanche to conduct my investigation . . . alone. They insisted on a certain discretion."

"Really . . . That's unusual."

"You're right, my friend, but one day you'll understand why, and you'll be the first to be satisfied. For now, rest, eat, drink, smoke your pipe, and read Dickens. There's nothing like it. I've got four weeks off; it won't take me that long to sort things out, but I'm also planning to allow myself a bit of leisure.

Triggs sighed; an hour later he filled his pipe and resumed reading *Nicholas Nickleby*.

ை

"Sigma-Tau . . . Have you heard of Freud, Breuer, and psychoanalysis?"[1]

"Not at all, Chief."

"Then let's not dwell on it; I don't know much about it either, but one of the axioms of this curious and learned theory is that at the source of the most audacious crimes is fear."

"That," Triggs murmured, "that . . . It doesn't take a great scientist to say or understand that."

"Indeed . . . Having said that, let's situate ourselves in Ingersham, or rather, in its neurosis."

"Huh? That's a difficult word."

"This neurosis is that of small provincial towns in general; I'm not saying there isn't something special about Ingersham, but let's not get ahead of ourselves. The small town's main occupations are eating, drinking, chatting, meddling in one's neighbor's business, and hating foreigners and anything likely to disturb the tranquility necessary for one's digestion and for profitable business.

"The reason for such trouble, Triggs, is the small city's neurosis, and here neurosis is synonymous with fear.

"Now, it so happens that one fine day, a policeman settles down in such a village."

"Not a policeman," grumbled Triggs, "a retired police secretary."

"But a policeman all the same in the eyes of good people; and just as the idea of a gun evokes that of a cartridge and vice versa, whoever says 'policeman' says crime and investigation. Why did he come? This is the question they asked in Ingersham."

Basket stood up and stared at the houses opposite.

"Inspector Triggs, which is the name they gave you here, thus settled in the main square. There is a view of the houses that I'm looking at; it is therefore their inhabitants who will be the first to ask themselves this question. They are the ones who, too, will be the first to worry."

"But what about?" Triggs inquired.

"We'll get to that, Sigma-Tau, but pay attention, I'm not going to follow a strict chronological order in explaining the mysteries that shook Ingersham, because some still retain their veils. It will be easy enough for me to drop them, but I'm a dilettante and am saving a few good bites for the end.

"Let's look at the house on the corner, that of the apothecary Pycroft.

"The druggist is one of the first to make overtures to you, to want to gain the confidence of the London policeman, in short, to want to know his plans which he foresees to be dark and dangerous."

"Dark and dangerous, what does that mean!" Triggs exclaimed.

"The evening passes in the most pleasant way and Pycroft is beginning to feel reassured . . ."

"Why wouldn't he have been?"

". . . when Doove starts telling one of his stories. Ah, Doove's stories, the role they've played in this vast provincial tragedy—and the one they'd have continued to play if Fate had not intervened with its scissors!"

"The story of Detective Repington . . ."

"Who never existed save in Doove's imagination!"

"Impossible! . . . And I claimed to know this famous man," lamented Triggs.

"There is no great harm. On the contrary, Sigma-Tau; you even went further by speaking in turn of a horrible and criminal reality: the crime of the famous Doctor Crippen.

"So, Pycroft knew enough, or so he believed. He committed suicide."

"But why? I never understood that suicide!"

"This morning, I explored the old apothecary's cellars; I had to dig under the flagstones . . . The corpse of Mrs. Pycroft was there, Triggs."

Sigma let out a moan of horror and grief.

"He had recognized himself in the criminal characters of the imaginary Colonel Crafton and the very real Doctor Crippen, evoked in turn by Doove and by you. Pycroft believed himself caught in a very subtle and devilish trap laid by the two of you. He rendered justice unto himself."

After a long silence, Humphrey Basket concluded:

"Each life has its mystery, one criminal, the other simply guilty, and few of Ingersham's inhabitants did not tremble at the arrival of the London policeman, believing him launched on the trail of this mystery whose discovery would forever ruin their lovely tranquility. Do you understand, Sigma-Tau? Such are the foundations of Ingersham's unspeakable fear."

"The Peully's water is rapidly subsiding," said Basket.

"Another mystery solved?" Triggs asked sarcastically.

"Unless you were satisfied with the conclusion to Freemantle's dismal story," Humphrey replied, giving him a taste of his own medicine.

"No, I admit it," Triggs confessed humbly.

"Basically, the tragic adventures of Freemantle and his neighbor Revinus stand as Siamese twins. Both loved Dorothy Chamsun ... Oh, I'm not saying that the lady wasn't playing a double game, but Revinus was a widower, Freemantle wasn't, and Miss Chamsun must have desired a husband above all. So she belonged entirely to the jovial baker; but, in the grip of the little town, they shrouded their liaison with all the mystery one could wish for. Freemantle, a crude man without much imagination, resorted to that pitiful pasquinade to achieve his ends.

"He doesn't seem to me to have been completely lacking in imagination, though," protested Triggs, "since he created the monster that haunted the Peully, and had a nameless terror reign there for I don't know how many years."

"Oh, is that what you believe? What if I told you that on the night your skill with the cane knocked him on his side, poor Freemantle had been playing the frightening character of the Bull for the first time?"

"What?" cried Triggs.

"Revinus and Dorothy Chamsun's affair was not a new one.

"Like all shy and jealous people, especially when the province also hangs over them, he spied on the couple, he took pleasure in tormenting himself with the sight of their happiness. Freemantle must have spent long night hours spying on the 'Purple Beeches,' eating his heart out as he followed the lovers while they exchanged sweet nothings in the darkness of the moor.

"And it was during these solitary stakeouts that he encountered *the true Bull*, the one actually terrifying the people of the Peully, the Travelers among others."

"Ah!" whispered Triggs, "so that's it . . ."

"I found the Travelers. They were camping on the border of Middlesex, on the edge of the flooded plains; I was able to gain their trust. Those poor folks have paid a truly horrible debt to the Peully monster, who stole from them and cut the throats of their children!"

"My God, and they didn't say anything about it."

"They were afraid of Chadburn," Basket answered simply; "the mayor of Ingersham definitely didn't want any trouble.

"This is horrible! We have to do something!" Triggs shouted.

"Come along, then," invited his former boss.

☙

Preceded by the harsh glare of a reflective lamp, the two policemen descended the spiral staircase leading to the subterranean passages of Ingersham city hall.

Triggs barely suppressed a shiver at seeing them so dark, so damp; a light icy rain was falling from the vaults; phosphorescent cryptogams gleamed faintly in the shadows; frightened by the light and the intrusion of men, rodents left their refuges, protesting sourly.

Basket pushed open a door and a polar breeze blew in their faces. The brightness of the reflective lamp was suddenly amplified by a violent refraction off large sparkling masses, in which Triggs recognized long blocks of ice.

"What is this?" he asked, bewildered.

"A makeshift morgue," Basket said.

Then Triggs saw a small, shriveled body lying on the flagstones.

"Try to recognize it," said Humphrey Basket softly, directing a jet of light at the motionless form.

Triggs saw a face of chalk green with empty eyes, framed by strange dark curls.

"I don't know her," he stammered . . . "Actually, wait, Basket, it seems . . . Oh! She looks like Queen Anne! You know, that bizarre portrait that served as a sign for the Pumkins ladies' shop!"

Basket pointed the reflective lamp at the corpse.

"Lady Florence Honnybingle," he said slowly.

Triggs cried out and, clinging to his friend's arm, begged him to end this nightmare.

Humphrey Basket leaned over the dead woman and abruptly pulled the long brown ringlets; Triggs heard the silky sound of tearing cloth and saw that his chief, as he raised his hand, held a wig.

"Look again."

Triggs didn't cry out this time: he no longer had the strength and, if his friend hadn't held him up, he would have collapsed on the miniature glacier.

He had recognized Deborah Pumkins.

"Drink! Swallow that rum for me. Is it too hot? Too bad, Triggs, it's the remedy you need to pull yourself together and listen to what I have to tell you about this new horror."

Sigma obeyed like a child; the toddy was indeed scalding, and tears welled up in his eyes; but he felt fortified all the same.

"And yet, Sigma-Tau," said Humphrey Basket suddenly, starting with a burst of nervous laughter, "you are the victor, the real one, this time, over the terror of the Peully!"

"How do you expect me to understand anything?" lamented the poor man.

"Who other than S. T. Triggs, at a memorable meeting of good neighbors, aided by the incomparable Mr. Doove, told the story of a great lady who had gone over to the side of crime and looked just like the Queen Anne of the sign of the hospitable house where he was being treated as a guest?"

"It was me . . ." whimpered Triggs. "But I didn't know . . ."

"To avoid causing great pain to a noble family, her name was never mentioned. A single file in the secret archives of the Yard mentions her: Lady Florence Honnybingle. At the end of her sentence, this damned woman was entrusted to her family, who vouched for her future conduct. Alas, crime held her in its sway . . . She evolved from a thief to a bloodthirsty monster and, with the aid of the fear of Ingersham and its mayor's obsession, she was able to move from one outrage to another with impunity."

"Her family," groaned Triggs, "her sisters . . ."

"No, her keepers, Sigma-Tau; the Pumkins ladies are not the sinister Lady's sisters. But do you understand why, after your dangerous chatter, they absconded? And why the sign disappeared which was only the family portrait of an ancestress who bequeathed to the criminal, in addition to her image, her formidable instincts?"

"Ruth Pumkins . . ." stammered Triggs; but Basket silenced him.

"Not all's yet been said," he said. "Don't get worked up, Sigma-Tau."

Suddenly, the latter raised trembling hands.

"The sign was removed around dawn . . ."

"And?" Basket asked.

"I don't know . . . I couldn't quite put into words what that made me think of; I thought those ladies couldn't get far."

"You're not so far from the truth, old man, but everything in its time, as our fathers said. On this subject, I must pay a debt to the memory of Miss Dorothy Chamsun; you almost did her a great injustice, Triggs, by suspecting her of attempting to murder you. The real culprit now lies on the icy slabs of the improvised morgue we've just left; you can easily understand the good reasons she had to put an end to a man as dangerous as you."

"But Ruth? . . ." insisted the unhappy policeman.

"I'm telling you, not all's yet been said, Sigma-Tau!"

✒

"Examine the calendar, Sigma, and tell us what time the full moon sets over Ingersham."

"Exactly at eleven-thirty, Chief."

"I sentence you to half a sleepless night, Triggs."

"We're going to . . . La Peully . . ." hesitated Sigma, his voice betraying no enthusiasm.

"Not at all; we're not leaving the neighborhood. We're going to take on the mystery of Cobwell, in particular."

Triggs counted on his fingers: the mystery of Pycroft, the mystery of Freemantle, the mystery of Revinus, the mystery of the Pumkins ladies, they had all melted away like wicked little snowmen in the sun.

"You remind me of a schoolmaster, Chief; in fact, he looked like Micawber in *David Copperfield*; he sweated profusely to teach us a little algebra and would always repeat in front of the mysterious equations on the blackboard: 'Let's proceed by elimination, gentlemen, eliminate . . . eliminate!'"

"Exactly; we shall proceed like your good schoolmaster, Sigma-Tau."

"We have two murders left . . ." Triggs said quietly.

"And a few flourishes . . . What time did we say that our friend the moon was making its roll call? Eleven thirty? We'll need to wait a bit; I only ordered the show for the age-old tradition: midnight."

Mrs. Snipgrass served a supper to which Basket alone did great credit.

"Time heals, as the country folk say," said Humphrey, emptying his jug of ale, "and soon the sun will gild this good little town of Ingersham again."

"Stripped of mystery," added Triggs regretfully, "will she be happier?"

"Mr. Squeers,[2] the schoolmaster of the delightful village of Dotheboys, near Greta Bridge in Yorkshire," joked Basket, "Mr. Squeers would certainly ask you if you are a philosopher and treat your remark as philosophy. But I answer it all the same: she would be less so if she were not left with the ghost of the city hall."

"Still?" Triggs exclaimed.

"And forever, Sigma-Tau!"

Triggs seemed to take great interest in the hard, green balls of peas on his plate, the sauce congealing between them, the jar of pickles, the pyramid of biscuits.

"Where are we going tonight?" he finally asked with an effort.

"To the art gallery where Gregory Cobwell died of fear, Sigma; I cannot wait to put you face to face with the frightful thing that caused his death."

"Lord, we still have some frightful things to see!" sighed the ex-policeman from Rotherhite. "For my part, I would gladly do without."

From the back of the garden came the snap of wooden shutters as the Snipgrasses sealed themselves off in their imminent sleep; from her doorstep, Mrs. Pilcarter called to her cat in a voice full of promises, then, having found him, she cursed him; in the sky, now clear again, the little inquisitive eyes of the stars resumed their eternal watch.

"How do we get into Cobwell's?" asked Triggs, alarmed. "After all, we can't break in; a warrant . . ."

"Tut-tut . . . let's not quibble. I knew that Mrs. Chisnutt had duplicate keys somewhere, which she naturally failed to put into the hands of Constable Lammle. I paid her a purely friendly visit, during which I promised not to conduct any investigation to recover the six cents' worth of fake antiquities she'd removed from the famous gallery. She handed me the keys and we parted lifelong friends. When I took leave of her, the good woman told me to beware of Suzan Summerlee, that devil made rather more of cardboard than fine modeling wax."

"Nonsense!" growled Triggs.

"I don't think so," said his former boss gravely.

The "Grand Art Gallery" had not undergone any changes; the footsteps of the two policemen raised only a little more dust than those of the late Cobwell had.

They settled on the plush sofa, and Basket turned off his flashlight. It was light enough: the moon was rising, and an eerie sea-green hue began to appear on the window curtains.

Triggs noticed that Suzan Summerlee's mannequin, still draped in her royal blue mantle, had not moved, and her shadow was beginning to look singularly sharp and fearsome.

The light increased; by this time the disc of the full moon was able to skim the walls of the garden. In the gallery, other forms took shape; in its niche, the dryad was shrouded in a ghostly mist; the dull helm of a shabby suit of armor peeked out.

"Midnight!"

The clock in the belfry counted out the fatal hour with exaggerated slowness.

Triggs suddenly felt a shiver and looked out the window: the curtain was billowing gently.

"The window has just been opened!" he whispered.

With a light touch of his hand, his companion urged him to be quiet.

He was just in time; a moment later and Triggs would have screamed in terror.

Suzan Summerlee, or rather her shadow, had just slowly raised her arm, and that arm was lifting an axe!

Basket didn't move, but his friend felt that he was fiercely following the spectral movement of the wax monstrosity.

Triggs could no longer keep calm and bear his inertia: the dummy, axe brandished, advanced toward them. He recoiled, a gasp of horror on his lips.

"Don't say a word, whatever you may see," Basket whispered to him; and he turned on the light.

Suzan Summerlee was three paces away, her ugly weapon raised to deliver the murderous blow.

But ... Triggs had to bite his lips till they bled to obey his boss: it wasn't the smiling face of Cobwell's wax dulcinea that was appearing in the light's yellow halo, but a pale mask, glistening with sweat, eyes closed, mouth twisted in anguish.

"Do nothing," Basket whispered in a barely audible breath, "she won't strike . . . she cannot. Leave her be!"

The terrifying form did in fact retreat toward the window and disappeared behind the curtains. As it left, Triggs saw the wax dummy, standing quietly in its place, smiling innocently.

"Did you recognize her?" Basket asked.

"Livina Chamsun!" groaned Triggs.

"That's why Cobwell died of fright," said Basket, "and if old Dr. Cooper hadn't told me that you had a stronger heart than the unfortunate master of the 'Grand Gallery,' I would have spared you that experience."

"Which has taught me nothing—on the contrary!"

"Bah! You're not such a layman as not to have recognized in Miss Chamsun a manifest case of somnambulism, if not of hypnosis.

"Shut the window, Triggs, and slide the bolt, though we need no longer dread a second visit from the strange intruder, and light the candles in this candelabrum, so that we can chat a little more comfortably. I'm going reveal to you the singular mechanism of the drama which put an end to the existence of Gregory Cobwell, a mechanism which also triggers another, and which will lead us to the end of all the mysteries of Ingersham."

$$\wp$$

"Bear with me here:

"The childish Gregory Cobwell, on that memorable afternoon, sunny and scorching, was busy annoying the world with his helio-teaser.

"The brightness of his apparatus wanders over a fenestra[3] of the city hall and brings daylight to a chamber which, until then, has escaped the attention of the antiques dealer.

"He sees something unusual that is worth a closer look; so, he immediately uses his powerful prismatic binoculars and sees . . .

"He sees the thing for which he'll have to die!

"And this thing is a leveling machine, a table and a hand that draws, and wads of counterfeit banknotes: Gregory Cobwell discovered, in the city hall of Ingersham, a counterfeiter's workshop.

"Cobwell is an honest man: he immediately senses what his duty is, but he has recognized the hand, and that hand belongs to a friend who frequents his house regularly, who shares his curious tastes as a collector, for whom, perhaps, he feels a vague tenderness."

"Livina Chamsun!"

"But on the other side of the street, they know what he has seen.

"They won't be leaving him alone.

"Cobwell hesitates, he thinks, argues with himself . . . or rather, he argues, as he usually does, with Suzan Summerlee, and he does so out loud.

"Through the window that a criminal hand is already opening, someone hears his soliloquy, learns his plans, and knows that he will wait until nightfall to go to the London policeman, the famous S. T. Triggs.

"Night comes, Cobwell makes up his mind, he will act . . .

"Livina Chamsun enters, draped in a dark mantle, an axe in her hand, and no doubt the very same play of shadows that for a moment made us accuse the inoffensive wax beauty threw Cobwell to the depths of terror.

"He had a weak heart, fear killed him . . ."

THE CITY OF UNSPEAKABLE FEAR

"Otherwise, Livina Chamsun's axe would have settled his account!" Triggs exclaimed in horror.

Basket waited a moment before answering.

"No," he said slowly, "no, she wouldn't have killed him, she couldn't have done it, just as she couldn't have lowered her axe to our heads. Livina Chamsun is not a criminal, Sigma-Tau! Let's say that fear has never served crime better . . . But I wonder if an infernal intelligence hadn't foreseen this thing!"

ᘒ

"Sigma-Tau?"

"I'm listening, Chief," Triggs said.

"Livina Chamsun certainly has her share of culpability in the work done in the tutelary shadow of the city hall. She is, in the eyes of the law, a delinquent; still I am inclined to minimize her responsibility; this unfortunate woman must have undergone an injurious influence, which significantly clouded her personality. Now, remember the two little acid burns . . ."

"On Doove's hands . . ." moaned Triggs. "Oh, I understand now. That great artist was also a great criminal: he was engraving fake banknotes! The master criminal, the mysterious crook who sowed terror with his insane stories, was the good Mr. Doove!!!"

"And yet he himself was murdered!"

"No doubt . . . An accomplice may have gotten rid of him."

"Miss Livina's axe shimmers horribly before your eyes, Triggs, and prevents you from seeing. It was indeed Doove who drew and engraved the precious figures, but he did so without realizing their corrupt destination.

"A skilled man can perfectly well order parts of motifs from an engraver, which he can then combine and assemble as he wishes. Which is what had been done.

"But old Doove wasn't altogether naïve, and the day you joked a little sharply about snaring him as a counterfeiter, he must have glimpsed the truth.

"He sought and found it.

"But he dared not confide in anyone, even through one of his clever stories. And what did he do? Well, what all inveterate story-tellers like him would have done: instead of telling it, he entrusted it to paper.

"I see very well what happened then: the infernal rascal who held Miss Chamsun through a sort of spell, who, more than likely, took recourse to hypnosis to make her a slave, and who had skill-fully used Doove's great talent, surprised him as he was writing his confession.

"He killed him and ... the rest you found for yourself, Sigma-Tau!"

"He killed him ... But you're going to end up accusing the ghost of hypnotizing young women and making dough!" Triggs protested vehemently.

"So you still cling to your ghost, my old friend," said Basket sadly. "Tell me . . . why play out the comedy?"

"The comedy?" stammered Triggs.

"Comedy," repeated Humphrey Basket firmly.

∽๛๏๛∽

"You're locked in the burgomaster cabinet with the mayor of Ingersham. Who are you waiting for? Or rather, who is Mr. Chadburn waiting for?

"You don't answer, Triggs, but I'll tell you: Chadburn is waiting for the ghost. It is perfectly possible that the ghost of the city hall will appear at the stroke of midnight. And then you, S. T. Triggs, the former devoted servant of the Metropolitan Police, will declare under oath that you have seen him; you won't dare deny, before the envoys of Scotland Yard, the existence of the strange creature from Beyond. And if the mayor claims he's convinced of the bloody guilt of the ghost, you won't dare contradict him!

"Don't protest, Triggs; you cannot do so, especially since there is already a ghost in your life, that of the execution victim Smauker!

"Oh, I'm not saying that poor Doove didn't foster this dreadful belief in your mind, nurtured by examples questionable or imaginary; but you are predestined to believe in ghosts, and Chadburn knew it.

"So you await the specter . . . which doesn't come, but in the meantime you play the role of your own little Doove, and you tell stories. And then someone, who had already been taking a very dim view of the arrival in Ingersham of a former London policeman, someone who has encountered you through various ins and outs and thought you by turns negligible and formidable as a detective, suddenly imagines that you are a policeman of merit on the trail of the mystery, and decides to finish you off.

"With you dead, he will either continue to accuse the phantom or take flight for good, that I could not say.

"You see a terrible face coming toward you from the depths of the darkness, you feel an iron hand resting on your neck . . .

"And you remember . . .

"You remember another hand that nearly broke your neck, just as it nearly broke mine.

"You remember, Triggs; and I'll tell you something else, *you recognize that odiously criminal hand*, that of Mike Sloop!!!"

Triggs rose. He was very calm, and his voice did not shake when he said:

"Inspector Basket, are you arresting me?"

♋

And Humphrey Basket replied:

"I will not arrest an honest and courageous man, who was acting in a case of self-defense.

"I will not arrest the man who saved my life.

"I will not arrest the man who rid society of Mike Sloop, an unrepentant criminal, even if he carved out a place for himself as one Mr. Chadburn, mayor of Ingersham.

"And, what's more, Sigma-Tau, I won't be arresting anyone in Ingersham, from whence the fear has fled for good.

"And my chiefs will be glad to see me take this course of action, Sigma-Tau."

♋

"Sigma-Tau?"

"I'm listening, Chief."

"Of whom or what are you thinking?"

"Of Livina Chamsun, Chief! Do you believe that Chadburn was able to suggest such criminal things to her? I thought that sort of thing was the stuff of novels."

"Hmm, not at all. Alas, such abominations exist! Chadburn, or Mike Sloop, to call him by his name, was a strong personality.

"I believe, moreover, that his hold over Livina Chamsun was one of a romantic nature: that unfortunate woman loved him, which must have strengthened the hold he had over her. But people acting under hypnosis rarely go so far as to commit a crime, and barely even hint at it.

"Also, as I told you, Livina *could not have killed*, but Sloop knew perfectly well that a great terror was enough to finish off Cobwell."

Basket jumped to his feet as if he had had enough of talking about horrors.

"The day is beautiful, Sigma-Tau. I want to take a walk along the Greeny, which has very quietly gone back to its bed."

They went along Broody Park and, as they reached the top of the gate, they saw Bill Blockson returning from fishing, a basket in hand.

"Is the fish in the bag, Bill?" Basket asked with a laugh.

"It is indeed, Sir, and two more in the trap."

The good man winked and went off in a good mood.

"Why doesn't he take them out of the trap?" asked Triggs.

"Probably because some species of fish don't interest him," Humphrey answered, pushing open the gate.

They entered the deserted park. The angry quarrels of jays and the staccato of blackbirds broke out.

"Look," said Triggs, "the red pavilion is open; it even looks inhabited."

As they approached the door, it opened.

"Come in, gentlemen!"

Triggs didn't come to his senses until he found himself in a neat and tidy little living room, next to Basket, who was nudging him, and two ladies who were smiling at him with a bit of embarrassment.

"Miss Patricia . . . Miss Ruth . . ."

"Come, Sigma-Tau, now it's time to drop the last veil of mystery, and you will understand why we must avoid adding a new stain to the sad memory of Lady Honnybingle.

"She was the granddaughter of Mr. Broody, your own benefactor, and the Pumkins ladies have been, for much of their lives, this noble gentleman's most devoted collaborators in trying to set her back on the right path. You mustn't blame them, Sigma Triggs, if they haven't always succeeded."

"We followed her in her . . . manias, to their most extreme limits, so as not to make her suffer too much," wept Miss Patricia; "but that's what Mr. Broody had wanted."

"And . . . Lady Honnybingle?" Triggs asked.

"She didn't want that name to disappear completely."

"Are we to discuss the strange designs of a madwoman?" Basket interrupted. "It would cost me the little Latin I have left.

"Let us always recall, as poor Mr. Doove did, our great Will where he proclaims that there are more things in heaven and earth than philosophers can dream of, and that too applies to the great fear of the ages, to the ghostly 'Them,' to the ghosts themselves . . .

"Enough, I say. By the way, Sigma-Tau, did you know that there is in Dickens, in *Bleak House*, a detective named Basket?"

But Triggs was no longer listening; he was talking in a low voice to Ruth Pumkins, whose cheeks had taken on a lovely rosy tint.

"Good," growled Humphrey, "and I dare bet a cannon against an old shoe that this will end like the adventure of Tim Linkinwater and Miss la Creevy."

Miss Patricia gave him a questioning look.

"It's in *Nicholas Nickleby*!" he explained.

THE CITY OF UNSPEAKABLE FEAR   165

"Ah! And may I ask you, Mr. Basket, how that adventure ends?"

"With a marriage . . ."

"That is indeed an adventure," said Miss Pumkins gravely, "but it's hard to say whether it's the ending of one or the beginning."

∽∾

"As for me," grumbled Humph Basket when he found himself alone in the park where the jays were screeching even louder, "I wonder if I must record this ending in my report. I can just imagine it one day falling into the hands of some damn young fellow who would make a fuss over it. There are plenty enough Mr. Dooves in this world . . ."

A Somber and Solitary Gentleman

A breath passes over the sets and characters of this story and takes away their existence and life. Time never acts otherwise, and the storyteller does the same.

Ingersham sleeps, weary of mysteries. The immense dreamless sleep of the small town has returned. In the high tower of the city hall, the clock begins to hum with all its cogs, about to strike midnight, its longest responsibility of the day.

The moon runs over the roofs with the cats, and the stars in their thousands make the Greeny a nocturnal mirror.

Twelve strikes . . . Tradition is the basis of eternal laws.

A moonbeam seeks passage through a stained-glass window and scatters the tiles of a corridor with fleeting silver.

A form begins to move, emerges from the shadows, and forms a train from the silvery ray.

It is perfectly human in its features and finery; yet it does not belong to this earth. It wears a robe, sabatons, and a bonnet, and a long tapering beard completes its honorable face.

This solitary gentleman would not inspire great fear were one to encounter him.

Yet he is a ghost, a real ghost, the only real one that has haunted Ingersham and will continue to do so, without interfering in the dramas of men.

He walks through closed doors and heavy stone walls, for his essence is subtle and mysterious.

167

He crosses with his even step, which is more like an ophidian slither than a human walk, the room where the Protector of the Poor decided to send obstinate royalists to a shameful death.[1] He pays no attention to the rigid seats that seem to drag out the fatal court session.

He enters the rich burgomaster cabinet where Mr. Chadburn's blood still stains the floor; he has no interest in this terrible evidence.

He passes through the glass-fronted office of the good Mr. Doove, without deigning to bend over his precious calligraphy, and when he reaches the round room from which the deceitful butterflies of counterfeit banknotes flew about the world, he doesn't pause.

He is indifferent to everything, and neither the happiness of men nor their sorrow shackles him.

What is the reason for this specter to wander through the night? Does such a reason even exist?

Has a boundless Wisdom, as interested in the futile life of a mite, in the quivering of a blade of grass as in the death of a world, assigned it a role?

To approach those after death, is it a strange privilege that this Wisdom refuses to living men, and if sometimes it befalls them, is it not an oversight of God himself?

Can an oversight be divine?

Are laws absolute?

Einsteinian science corroded the brass of Euclid like a perverse acid; polarization shocks the radiant code of optics, the intransigence of the equilibrium of liquids is defeated by capillarity, and learned men have forged catalysis from scratch, to save themselves from ignorance.

Of divine legislation, the Churches have rounded off many angles; to the axioms of God were born, like buds, human corollaries.

Then the law of the night gave birth to crevices through which ghosts could slip.

We have made Nature a truth like God; in fact, it teems with mirages and lies.

Bah! . . . Words, nothing but words! . . . Ah! Shakespeare!

Forms or forces, something takes the place of the dead, but these forms bow to no plan and it is difficult to calculate in *poncelets* the power of the forces of the night.

The ghost is.

It prowls, wanders, comes and goes.

The rooster crows; he disappears.

Tradition.

THE END

TRANSLATOR'S AFTERWORD

F for Fear

Director Jean-Pierre Mocky's 1964 film adaptation of *La cité d'indicible peur*, originally released as *La grande frousse* ("The Big Scare" or "The Great Fright"), begins with Inspector "Simon Triquet," played by the popular French singer and comedic actor Bourvil, traveling down a colonnaded avenue with his peculiar half-running, half-skipping gait. It is night, and Triquet interacts with various fellow police officers along his way. The scene is an obvious, if abbreviated, recreation of the opening of Orson Welles's 1958 film noir classic *Touch of Evil*, in which Inspector Ramon Miguel Vargas (Charlton Heston) and his new bride Susan (Janet Leigh) take a similar stroll along the US–Mexico border crossing between Ciudad Juárez and El Paso. Although Welles's version is far more complex and includes an exploding car, the homage is inescapable (and Mocky's admiration for Welles is a matter of record). Perhaps parody is a better word than homage; in fact, Mocky's film seems at times almost a parody of the original novel.

In an intriguing coincidence, Orson Welles himself went on to play a major role in the next major film adaptation of Jean Ray's work, Harry Kümel's 1971 *Malpertuis*. Welles portrayed one of the most important characters in Ray's oeuvre, the dying wizard Cassavius (Cassave in the novel). Kümel and others later claimed that Welles was drunk and rude on the set and insisted on directing himself, although other evidence, including actual outtakes, disputes these claims. The truth of these events remains elusive, as does so much in the lives of both Jean Ray and Orson Welles.

Three years after *Malpertuis*, in 1974, Welles released the last film he completed in his lifetime, one of his finest and almost certainly his funniest:

F for Fake, a quasi-documentary ostensibly about the prolific art forger Elmyr de Hory and the author Clifford Irving, who is best remembered for his hoax biography of Howard Hughes, but who also published a biography of de Hory in 1969: *Fake: The Story of Elmyr de Hory, the Greatest Art Forger of Our Time*. Welles drew extensively on footage from an earlier documentary that showed Irving interviewing de Hory, arguably capturing the moment when the author realized he could profitably apply de Hory's problematic craft to his own medium. In the film, Welles acknowledges that Howard Hughes, rather than William Randolph Hearst, was the original intended subject of *Citizen Kane*. Much of the content of the film is at least partially, and openly, "fake" in some way, and the final sequence, involving Pablo Picasso, Welles's partner Oja Kodar, and another art forger, is ultimately revealed as a complete charade. The entire film functions as a visual essay on the nature of fakery, authorship, charlatanism, and expertise. Two years after the release of *F for Fake*, Elmyr de Hory, fearing prosecution in France, committed suicide, much like the apothecary Pycroft in this novel: life imitating art at the end of a life of imitating art.

The City of Unspeakable Fear is a novel full of fakes, forgeries, inferior copies, false identities, and impersonations. Sometimes these accumulate on top of each other: a counterfeit mayor running a real counterfeiting operation; a real woman impersonating a wax mannequin that once portrayed a real-life axe murderer; a monstrous noblewoman living in disguise who reveals her true self in the guise of a monster. If the accumulating coincidences and serendipities of its unfolding plotline seem at times a tad outlandish, they are hardly more so than some of those in the sequence of real-life events I have described above.

The novel even begins with a false start: an ominous unnumbered preliminary chapter that opens in the fourteenth century with Geoffrey Chaucer encountering a spectral horde while on the lam in Southwark. This opening then carries us through various sinister and bloody bits of the UK's history from Wat-Tyler and Anne Boleyn to Jack the Ripper and the Loch Ness Monster. Here we can see Ray entering his Chaucer period (he titled his next collection, released the following year, *The Last Canterbury Tales*). Although Ray's devotion to Dickens remains most obvious herein, Chaucer's influence is nonetheless apparent in the novel's episodic structure, comprised of various tales: the Policeman's, the *Scabin*'s, the Apothecary's, the Storeowner's, the Maid's, etc., as well as the way these stories sometimes descend into other internal stories as many as three levels deep.

One may also detect an overall homage to Arthur Conan Doyle's *The Hound of the Baskervilles*, the novel in which Dr. Watson serves as the protagonist throughout most of the story rather than Sherlock Holmes, who arrives near the end to explain away the supernatural elements and reveal the true culprits—just as Humphrey Basket does in *The City of Unspeakable Fear*. However, although Jean Ray wrote over a hundred stories of "Harry Dickson, the American Sherlock Holmes," he gives this novel of detectives and terror on the British moors a flavor more Dickensian than Sherlockian, which is apparent not only in the numerous allusions to Dickens but in the wonderfully off-kilter character names: Chickenbroker, Slumbot, Sloop, Snugg, Pumkins, Basket, Blockson, Ebenezer Doove, Lady Florence Honnybingle . . . Only in the penultimate chapter do we get a taste of the elegant ratiocination typical of the tales of either Sherlock Holmes or Harry Dickson.

More than anything, however, this novel is Ray's tribute to the UK, a nation he apparently never visited except in his imagination, but for which he clearly held a special admiration. Here the British setting allows him to indulge that admiration to the fullest, invoking Oliver Cromwell, brownies, the moors, a host of his favorite British authors, and an assortment of historical incidents and locales, both real and imagined, creating a *mise-en-scène* that Arnaud Huftier, the preeminent Jean Ray scholar, aptly describes in his own afterword to the most recent French edition as "more British than British" (*plus british que british*).

Into this panorama of actual British history and culture, Ray weaves his own pseudohistorical narrative about a plague of murderous phantoms that periodically strikes the UK. He refers to the almost-invisible entities that compose this plague, so very similar to the otherworldly vampires in his novella "The Gloomy Alley," only as THEM (sometimes in all capital letters, sometimes in italics, occasionally in quotes). This creates a minor problem for the translator, as the French *ils* can mean either "them" or "they" depending on context, while the corresponding English pronoun has different forms in the subject and object cases (while translating this novel, I empathized with William Olivier Desmond, who translated Stephen King's *IT* into French, a language that lacks a third-person singular neuter pronoun: Desmond opted for *ÇA*, French for *THAT*). Jean Ray's THEY, given a false historical grounding by the real historical and geographical context in which he embeds them, provide the ostensible source of the Unspeakable Fear that comes to Ingersham.

After this brief opener, so replete with pronouns, phantoms, and foreshadowing, the actual narrative commences—though not without something of a second false start. Ray delays the first act once more to introduce us to the novel's protagonist, Sidney Terence "Sigma-Tau" Triggs, who "was never a policeman," and the first half of the chapter presents us with a short biography of this "detective in spite of himself," focusing on the rather limited high points of his official career in law enforcement. Only with Triggs's retirement to his old hometown of Ingersham does the novel's primary narrative arc truly get underway. Meanwhile, the reader must decide which of the elements of the first one and a half chapters are Chekhov's guns and which are red herrings.

In the introduction, I invited the reader to consider whether *The City of Unspeakable Fear* is a detective novel or a horror novel, a question posed on the cover of the 1971 paperback edition from Marabout. This ambiguity in presentation goes back to the original 1943 edition published by Les

Auteurs Associés, whose editors included the volume in their lineup of detective novels but packaged it as a horror novel with macabre illustrations. The tension between these two possible readings, augmented by the overlay of sometimes cartoonish dark humor, is in large part the source of the novel's enduring charm. All these categories must have offered some level of escapism during the Nazi occupation of Belgium, a time when readers surely would have welcomed even temporary alternatives to reality.

The case for viewing the novel as a detective novel (*un roman policier*) seems fairly clear at first: after all, the protagonist *is* a detective. Or is he? The first line of the first chapter tells us Sigma Triggs was never a policeman. He identifies himself as "a retired police secretary." In the first chapter, Ray politely portrays him as an incompetent traffic cop who was reassigned to a desk job, for which his exemplary penmanship fortunately suited him well. Besides his fine scribal hand, Triggs's only other notable skill as a policeman is his proficiency with a billy club (or any expedient substitute), which we do not learn about until Chapter V. His entire career has only two memorable moments: the identification and arrest of the murderer Bunny Smauker and saving his chief from strangulation at the hands of the counterfeiter Mike Sloop. And then he is put out to pasture. It is only after his arrival in Ingersham that the townspeople mistakenly identify him as "Inspector Triggs," and he allows this imposture to continue out of a mix of shyness and pride.

Triggs is no Sherlock Holmes, no Harry Dickson, no Jules Maigret, no Hercule Poirot. He is not, however, a bumbler—except when directing traffic. Nor is he a coward, as we see in his encounters with Mike Sloop and the Bull of the Peully. He has, as discussed, certain skills, and he once noticed the telltale identifying marks of a murderer that his colleagues had missed. Indeed, he is perceptive, though only up to a point: time and again in *The City of Unspeakable Fear* Triggs makes casual observations that are close enough to hidden truths to incite genuine panic in those around him.

He is a "detective in spite of himself." Moreover, he is not the only detective in the novel: Humphrey Basket arrives at the denouement and brings a truly professional acumen to bear on the violent and seemingly incomprehensible events of Ingersham. Thus, the case for the novel as a detective novel rests on a sound foundation.

Or are we dealing here with a horror novel (*un roman d'épouvante*)? The opening chapter certainly suggests that it might be, with its mysterious and murderous pronominal phantoms and its references to Jack the Ripper, the Loch Ness Monster, banshees, and brownies. After all the pains Ray takes to establish their historicity, his mysterious THEY remain offstage for the rest of the novel, appearing only in the terrified minds of Ingersham's inhabitants. We do encounter a child-murdering serial killer, Lady Florence Honnybingle, but the full scope of her hideous activities is only hinted at, briefly, near the novel's end.

What, then, is *The City of Unspeakable Fear*? It is certainly not another *Malpertuis*. Arnaud Huftier suggests that while "*Malpertuis* is mysterious, even hermetic . . . *The City of Unspeakable Fear* is almost grand-guignolesque, if not parodic."[1] In *La grande frousse*, director Jean-Pierre Mocky—and screenwriters Gérard Klein (one of France's most important science fiction authors) and Raymond Queneau (avant-garde icon and cofounder of Oulipo)—chose to lean into the dark humor that is inherent in the novel and in much of Ray's early work, especially in some of the darkly ironic stories depicting the criminal underworld in *Whiskey Tales* (here we get the story from the police perspective).

Mocky's film is comedy verging on slapstick combined with elements of the absurd that approach the surreal. He received initial criticism for these choices and for his casting of Bourvil, but these choices are valid, as they play to the novel's strengths rather than attempting to frame it as a darker and more gothic narrative. Though such an approach might have fit the expectations of Ray's readers at the time (and since), it would have required an even greater distortion of the original story. It does remain tempting, however, to imagine a Hammer Films production of this novel, something along the lines of the 1959 version of *The Hound of the Baskervilles* starring Peter Cushing and Christopher Lee—or, for that matter, Harry Kümel's *Malpertuis*. Nonetheless, we cannot look to *La grande frousse* to define the genre of the novel, which, although it expands the humorous and irrational aspects of the story, also maintains its mixture of mystery and horror.

There is a popular misconception that *The City of Unspeakable Fear* is not a true novel at all, but instead merely a "fix-up" of several Harry Dickson stories repackaged as a long-form narrative. This interpretation does not hold up upon examination. Sigma Triggs is almost the antithesis of the masterful and resourceful Dickson, so much so as to suggest that Ray may have created him as a deliberate alternative to his more famous detective, perhaps even as his version of killing off Holmes at the Reichenbach Falls. Harry Dickson was, after all, a literal derivative of Arthur Conan Doyle's iconic character, having begun as an explicit imitation thereof ("The American Sherlock Holmes"). Various versions of an "Inspector Triggs" appear in Ray's stories in Dutch (and two in French), but these characters are genuine detectives, something Ray tells us Sigma Triggs is not in the first line of the first chapter of *The City of Unspeakable Fear*. Nor do these early Triggs characters ever use the name "Sigma Triggs." Same surname; very different characters. These earlier versions are all real police inspectors, largely interchangeable variations among the many recurring detectives in Ray's earlier work, including not only Triggs and Harry Dickson but Edmund Bell, Jack Linton, and Inspector Wheeler.

The primary connection between the Harry Dickson stories and *The City of Unspeakable Fear* is that Ray had already used a very similar title, *La cité de l'étrange peur*, for a Dickson story in 1937. A genuine overlap exists between these two works, but it is almost entirely based on a single shared scene: the Pumkins ladies' tea party in Chapter IV of the novel. Several paragraphs of this episode occur almost verbatim in both texts, including the comical argument over the menu between Patricia Pumkins and Molly Snugg (Deborah Hasslop and Molly Vinck in the earlier novella). Many of the guests have the same or similar names, and Mr. Doove appears at first to be the same character. Chadburn plays a role, but only as a minor police character with no similarity to his counterpart in this novel. A version of the subplot involving Lady Florence Honnybingle features importantly in the Dickson novella, and the scenes where Molly sees her in the usually empty armchair are almost identical. The two works diverge wildly after that, however, with the Dickson novella taking wild turns through dead men with green skin, bigamy (Doove turns out to be a ship captain who is simultaneously married to *all* the women at the tea party), and a very different version of Lady Florence Honnybingle, who is actually a former princess, priestess, and pirate from the Polynesian island of Raratonga who controls a London borough of mostly empty houses and keeps it free of (other) criminals through the use of deadly electric catfish. The two stories may share one key scene and versions of several characters, but *La cité de l'étrange peur* takes off on a wild pulpy ride that bears no relation to *The City of Unspeakable Fear*. Reading both, one may suspect that either the Dickson novella is the more recent of the two, or that both narratives recycled a common fragment that was itself the survivor of some earlier unpublished project.

In addition to the various earlier uses of the name "Triggs" and that one shared scene with some similar characters and names, one can find a few other faint echoes of *The City of Unspeakable Fear* elsewhere in Ray's sprawling oeuvre. This is not unusual *chez* Ray: we know, for instance, that several of his major works, including *Malpertuis*, derive at least in part from an earlier unfinished manuscript entitled "Aux lisières des ténèbres" ("On the margins of darkness"). His work is also full of recurring characters: the aging sorcerer, the three spinster sisters, the sinister taxidermist with the pear-shaped head. Because Ray's notebooks and manuscripts have been almost entirely lost, it is all but impossible to determine the first appearance and/or evolution of any element in his work. Yet despite its tenuous connections to an assortment of minor works, *The City of Unspeakable Fear* is a fully original creation, unique in Ray's oeuvre, and arguably on a larger scale. It is a novel that invites the reader to question not only the characters and events of its narrative, but also its own nature—and ultimately, the nature of reality itself. Yet it does so without the least degree of pretentiousness.

By setting his novel in an English country town, Ray effortlessly establishes for the reader that we are in a location where things are to be taken at face value and people are just who they seem to be and say they are. This is, after all, the superficial way of small towns. Of course, anyone who has actually lived in such a town for any length of time will recognize immediately how much of a fiction this is. From hidden secrets to concealed identities, Ingersham is a town of still waters that run deep, a point that the landscape itself emphasizes when the placid Greeny rises in a raging flood and drowns several major characters.

In addition to these elements, and to an array of objective correlatives including the obvious forgeries and the poor-quality wax model of the Grand Cobwell Art Gallery, Ray also presents us with Mr. Doove's elaborately fabricated narratives and a series of characters with hidden secrets and assumed identities. Ultimately, at the center of it all, we find a phony mayor and a very real counterfeiting operation. Even our protagonist is a fraud, though involuntarily so: the townspeople quickly dub retired police secretary Sigma Triggs *Inspector* Triggs, an active detective of Scotland Yard. This final and intrusive imposture is the one that causes most of the others to unravel.

This profusion of imitations, especially the cheap copies in Cobwell's art gallery and Mike Sloop/Mayor Chadburn's counterfeit operation, evokes Walter Benjamin's canonical 1935 essay "The Work of Art in the Age of Mechanical Reproduction." Although I am not suggesting that Ray read this text (he easily may have, as a French edition was available by 1936), both

Benjamin's essay and this novel belong to the same zeitgeist of a darkly and justifiably fearful time and represent different ways of considering related questions about the encroachment of modernity on older, more traditional lifeways. Benjamin also provides an excellent framework for comparing *The City of Unspeakable Fear* with *Malpertuis*: "Humanity, once, in Homer, a spectacle for the gods of Olympus, has now become one only for itself" ("Die Menschheit, die einst bei Homer ein Schauobjekt für die Olympischen Götter war, ist es nun für sich selbst geworden"). One might fairly describe *Malpertuis* as the final moment of transition when the Olympians go from observing humanity to becoming a fading spectacle themselves, while *The City of Unspeakable Fear*, is, in turn, all about a flawed humanity regarding—and misunderstanding—itself.

Just as this novel is full of fakes, forgeries, impersonations, and misunderstandings, it is full of fears as well, from the great fear that grips the entire town and the monster that terrorizes the Travelers camped on Ingersham's moor, the Peully, to the far more personal fears that so many of Triggs's new neighbors hold of their secrets being uncovered: a fear of the truth. The plot of the novel thus derives from the interplay of fakery and fear, as the fears that motivate its characters are the products of misunderstandings and mistakes, primarily the false assumption that Triggs, a retired failed traffic cop, was an active Scotland Yard detective; the failure to plumb the truth about Lady Florence Honnybingle and the child-murdering Bull of the Peully; and the misattribution of Ingersham's multiplying tragedies to THEM. At one point Ebenezer Doove relates one of his bogus stories, a narrative of the fictitious detective Maple Repington. The telling of this tale, which combines elements of Sherlock Holmes, Bluebeard, and Edgar Allan Poe's "The Telltale Heart," contributes to the suicide of the apothecary Pycroft. In the end, however, Humphrey Basket explains away most of the novel's supernatural elements, placing *The City of Unspeakable Fear* largely in the category of "Weird Menace," a variation of the Weird Tale once popular in the heyday of the pulp magazines, in which everything outré is ultimately subject to rational explanation. Today we might call this a "Scooby-Doo ending," and indeed the novel includes a scene just like the iconic endings of the venerable cartoon (first broadcast in 1969), in which Triggs unmasks the Bull as Freemantle the butcher.

To be sure, Humphrey Basket never offers an explanation for "THEY/THEM." As They never actually manifest in Ingersham, he doesn't need to. They remain a mystery at the novel's end, although Ray took pains to present them as genuine at the beginning. The other supernatural entity that Basket does not explain away is the ghost that haunts Ingersham's city hall. Instead, the detective acknowledges its existence, and in the novel's short final chapter, Ray takes this a step further. This ghost, however, never becomes a figure of horror, even though Mayor Chadburn/Mike Sloop attempts to portray it as responsible for the murder of Ebenezer Doove.

The closest "They" come to appearing in the novel after the opening is when the townspeople mistakenly identify the Travelers fleeing the Peully from the supposed horde of spectral murderers. Ironically, the Travelers are fleeing both "Them," which they "feel," and the very real Bull, the monstrous avatar of Lady Florence Honnybingle, who has been murdering their children. Jean Ray does not forget "Them," however. As Inspector Basket begins the novel's protracted denouement, Triggs asks: "They've come from Scotland Yard?" and his chief replies: "*They* haven't come . . . only *me*." Through this simple linguistic subversion (which fortunately works the same in English), "They," the source of the great fear, are reduced and ultimately replaced by the forces of law and order, neatly balancing out a process that began when the arrival of Sigma Triggs in Ingersham initiated a cycle of fear and death.

Although the spectral menace of THEY/THEM is altogether Ray's own creation, there are genuine historic analogues for the great fear that came to Ingersham. Indeed, numerous events of mass panic or hysteria are documented on every continent, from the Dancing Plague of 1518 to

Spring-Heeled Jack and the Mad Gasser of Mattoon. Interestingly, Ray never mentions the Great Fear that swept France in 1789, at the start of the Revolution, perhaps because that event never held any supernatural associations. One of the most obvious examples, and one that Ray would certainly have been familiar with, was the terror caused by the Beast (or Beasts) of Gévaudan from 1764 to 1767, during which one or more large wolf-like animals killed as many as five hundred people in southern France. Scholars still dispute the exact nature of the several large animals killed during this period, which may have been wolves, hybrid wolfdogs, striped hyenas, or even thylacines somehow imported to France from eastern Oceania. A very similar reign of terror occurred far more recently, when entities variously reported as wolves, werewolves, or Pakistani paramilitary agents disguised as wolves killed over thirty children in the Indian state of Uttar Pradesh during the 1990s.

Of course, we cannot omit Orson Welles's legendary Panic Broadcast of 1938: Welles's greatest fake was also a "great fear." More respected during his lifetime in the Francophone world than in his own country, the legendary director "made his bones" when he was only twenty-three years old through his now-legendary production of Howard Koch's radio adaptation of H. G. Wells's novel *The War of the Worlds*, which caused listeners within its broadcast area to panic, thinking that the events Welles was narrating as if he were a news announcer were true.

The resonance of the Panic Broadcast registered fully on me during the late spring of 2022, when I visited Grovers Mill, New Jersey, together with my partner, author Anya Martin. Grovers Mill is an unincorporated community of Colonial vintage, located in West Windsor Township south of Princeton. Either West Windsor or Grovers Mill proper would serve eminently well as the setting for an American film version of *The City of Unspeakable Fear*. Despite heavy rain, we were able to visit a series of recently installed historical markers commemorating the broadcast in a local park, as well as a moderately avant-garde metal sculpture of one of the Martian tripods from Wells's novel. A smallish, conical water tower at which locals supposedly fired shots on the night of the broadcast still stands, but we were unable to see this owing to summer foliage. Almost a century later, the "great fear" that Welles invoked with a single forty-minute radio broadcast remains deeply embedded in popular culture and social memory, more so than many actual events. To be sure, the effectiveness of Welles's *The War of the Worlds* was almost certainly amplified by growing fears of a German invasion, just as H. G. Wells's original novel benefited from similar fears in the UK when it was first serialized in 1897 (and George Pal's 1953 film version obviously drew on Cold War paranoia). Less than two years after the Panic Broadcast, in May 1940, Nazi Germany invaded Belgium, Ray's homeland. *The City of Unspeakable Fear* was published during the occupation, together with *Malpertuis* and several of the author's other major works.

Although "They" never appear in *The City of Unspeakable Fear* beyond the opening, at the novel's end, Ray presents us with a brief coda, the portrait of "a somber and solitary gentleman." This gentleman is the ghost that haunts Ingersham's city hall, "a real ghost, the only real one that has haunted Ingersham and will continue to do so, without interfering in the dramas of men." The appearance of a genuine supernatural element after everything else in a narrative has received a rational explanation, has, as a trope, become something of a cliché nowadays, especially in the cinema, but it still retained some freshness in 1943. In this final chapter, Ray returns to cosmic horror, in particular the unique brand thereof that makes his work so different from most of his Anglophone contemporaries. With Jean Ray, the Weird juxtaposes the inhuman cosmology of Einsteinian physics with Judeo-Christian mythology in a universe where both operate, though with an ever-increasing tension between them. Here, just as elsewhere in his work, the cosmic horror appears to derive not from realms uncovered by the strange new discoveries of astronomers and physicists, but from the vast indifference of the divine creator. Ray suggests that this interplay between the realms of Einstein and God "gave birth to crevices through which the ghosts could slip." Ultimately, he concludes first that "nature teems with mirages and lies" and then that all his previous conclusions are "words, nothing but words."

At the end of a novel in which most of the supernatural elements have been explained away as fictions and many human identities are exposed as frauds, the only reality is a ghost that turns out to be not only indifferent to human affairs, but oblivious to them altogether.

What then are we to make of *The City of Unspeakable Fear*? Is it a detective novel, a horror novel—both—or a legitimate example of neither? Can we accept that it is not a fake, a fix-up, or some unholy union, but a unique hybrid of both forms, along with the addition of elements uncommon to either? It may just be that Raymundus Joannes de Kremer, who spent two years in prison for fraud, whose major works included his own wildly sensationalized and almost entirely fictional autobiography, and who employed more than two dozen pseudonyms during his career (of which Jean Ray is only the best known), authored a brilliant and finely crafted hybrid novel, which three decades before Orson Welles's final masterpiece offered its own extended meditation on truth, fiction, authorship, and identity, once again bypassing modernism and coming by a crooked road directly into postmodernism, just as he had done in *Malpertuis*.

NOTE

1. Jean Ray, *La cite de l'indicible peur* (Paris: Alma, éditeur, 2016), 235.

TRANSLATOR'S NOTES

OPENING: "THEM . . ."

1. John Wycliffe (ca. 1320s–1384) was a fourteenth-century English religious dissident whose critique of Catholicism made him an important forerunner of the Protestant Reformation. He taught Chaucer at Oxford in 1367. Chaucer, in turn, paid tribute to Wycliffe in lines 479–530 of the Prologue to *The Canterbury Tales*.

2. Hainaut is today a province of Wallonia and Belgium, known in English as Heynowes. A significant portion of what was once the medieval county of Hainaut is now part of France. In Chaucer's time, the entire county belonged to a branch of the Wittelsbach dynasty.

3. Located on the south bank of the Thames, Southwark is South London's oldest district. Although settlement there dates back to Roman times, its importance derives in large part from its position at the southern terminus of the old London Bridge. Chaucer's pilgrims begin their journey from an historical inn there, The Tabard. Later, Southwark became the location of both Philip Henslowe's The Rose and later the Globe Theatre, both associated with Shakespeare.

4. Walter "Wat" Tyler (ca. 1320/1324 or 1341–1381) led the 1381 English Peasants' Revolt. His rebel forces marched from Canterbury to London in opposition of a poll tax and demanded reforms. The rebellion was initially successful but ended badly for the rebels after officers of King Richard II killed Tyler during negotiations at Smithfield, London. Ray's confusing reference to the "rebellion of 1640" may refer to the Second Bishops' War. Wat-Tyler had been dead almost three centuries by that time.

5. Carlisle is a border city in North West England, located at the confluence of the Eden, Caldew, and Petteril rivers.

6. Samuel Podgers was a fictional occult scholar created by Ray. His name also appears in the novella "The Great Nocturnal." Ray likely derived the name from a combination of two characters in Charles Dickens's "Mr. Pickwick's Tale": Samuel Pickwick and John Podgers.

7. Now the administrative center of Lancashire, England, Preston is an ancient city on the north bank of the River Ribble. Bonnie Prince Charlie, the Jacobite Prince, rested his army in Preston in December of 1745 prior to their final, tragic retreat that ended on Culloden Moor.

I SIDNEY TERENCE OR SIGMA TRIGGS

1. A venerable town in the Rushmoor district of Hampshire, England, Aldershot is located southwest of London. The establishment there of the Aldershot Garrison in 1854 led to a close and ongoing association with the British Army. Soldiers from the Garrison encountered Spring-Heeled Jack in 1877.

2. The *Anabasis* (in Greek Ἀνάβασις: "embarkation" or "expedition up from") is the best-known work of Xenophon (ca. 430–354 BCE). This seven-volume narrative describes the expedition of a large force of Greek mercenaries enlisted by Cyrus the Younger when he sought to seize the throne of Persia from his brother, Artaxerxes II, in 401 BCE. Xenophon likely composed the seven books of the *Anabasis* ca. 370 BCE.

3. Samuel Pickwick is the protagonist of Charles Dickens's first novel, *The Pickwick Papers* (1836). The character's name probably derives from Eleazer Pickwick, a prominent British businessman (ca. 1749–1837). A gallant but naïve and ineffectual character, Pickwick provides continuity to the episodic structure of Dickens's novel just as Sigma Triggs does here. This is the first of many allusions to Dickens's oeuvre in *The City of Unspeakable Fear.*

4. Part of the tideway of the Thames, the Pool of London is a stretch of the Thames from London Bridge to below Lime House. The Pool was divided into two parts: the Upper Pool, comprising the section between London Bridge and the Tower Bridge, and the Lower Pool, from the Tower Bridge to Cherry Garden Pier in Rotherhithe.

5. Ingersham is entirely Ray's creation, but this reference to its location places it somewhere southeast of modern London. Middlesex County no longer exists today as a political entity, having been absorbed by Greater London, a process that began as early as the twelfth century and was completed in 1965.

6. Robert Nixon, the legendary "Cheshire prophet." Conflicting accounts place his life anywhere between the late fifteenth and early seventeenth centuries. His alleged prophecies were most widely circulated in pamphlets published during the eighteenth century. Among other things, he is claimed to have predicted the popularity of cigarettes ("All sorts will have chimneys in their mouths").

7. HM Prison Pentonville (a.k.a. "The Ville") is not actually located in Pentonville, but further north in the London Borough of Islington. After the closure of the infamous Newgate Prison in 1902, Pentonville became the execution site for north London.

8. Épinal is a commune in northeastern France, particularly well-known for the *images d'Épinal*, prints produced there by the Imagerie Pellerin. These prints— stencil-colored woodcuts largely depicting naively idealized scenarios based on military subjects, Napoleonic history, and folklore themes—became so popular in France in the nineteenth century that the name of the commune became synonymous with them in French. The company that produced them, now the Imagerie d'Épinal, is still in operation, and continues to print the images with its historic hand-operated presses.

9. Another allusion to Dickens and to *Nicholas Nickleby* specifically. The multiple references to Dickens in this novel support the hypothesis of its early composition, as it is Ray's first two collections, *Whisky Tales* and *Cruise of Shadows*, where he pays the most abundant homage to Dickens.

10. Presumably Eduard Hildebrandt (1818–1868), a German landscape painter originally famous for his Parisian street scenes. He traveled around the world in 1864–1865 and in his last years became known for painting "exotic" scenes from his travels.

11. The *Sotie* was a type of short satirical play popular in France in the fifteenth and sixteenth centuries, featuring companies of fools (*sots*) attired in the traditional costumes thereof.

12. Robert Southey (1774–1843) was an English Romantic poet, considered something of a sellout by his peers. He served as poet laureate from 1813 until the time of his death and is primarily remembered today as the author of the earliest published version of the story of Goldilocks and the Three Bears.

13. Scottish poet and author Tobias George Smollett (1721–1771) published his *History of England* between 1760 and 1765 as a continuation of David Hume's earlier four-volume *History of England* (1757–1758), with Smollett picking up from the reign of William and Mary and ending with the death of George II. Smollett's work was also an important influence on some of Ray's greatest models, especially Charles Dickens and Laurence Sterne.

II   MR. DOOVE TELLS SOME STORIES

1. Ray alludes here to Saint Adelbert's curse or charm against thieves, which appears in several magical books. The text as it appears here seems to be

largely Ray's own version, bearing only a general resemblance to the original in either English or French.

2. Although this ill-fated magistrate appears to be Ray's confabulation, the story that Doove relates contains elements of Joseph Sheridan Le Fanu's 1872 novelette "Mr. Justice Harbottle."

III GAMES OF THE SUN AND THE MOON

1. The renowned architect and scientist Christopher Wren (1632–1723).

2. The Roman architect and engineer Vitruvius (ca. 80–70 BCE–after ca. 15 BCE), author of *De architectura*. His principles of *firmitas*, *utilitas*, and *venustas* (strength, utility, and beauty) provided the basis for Leonardo da Vinci's famous sketch of the Vitruvian Man.

3. Mary Pearcey (1866–1890) was an Englishwoman convicted of murdering her lover's wife, Mrs. Phoebe Hogg, and child, Tiggy, on 24 October 1890. She was hanged for those crimes on 23 December of that same year. Pearcey has been suggested as a possible Jack the Ripper suspect (and was the only female suspect considered at the time of the murders). The case was a sensational one in its day, so much so that Madame Tussauds of London inevitably added a wax figure of Pearcey. The museum also purchased the bloody perambulator employed as evidence in the trial. The noose with which Pearcey was executed remains on display at the Black Museum of Scotland Yard, a detail appropriate to this novel.

4. *Caput mortuum* (Latin: literally "dead head" or "worthless remains") refers to the exhausted residues of alchemical activities.

5. Vernet was the surname of three generations of French painters, beginning with Claude-Joseph Vernet (1714–1789), best known for his seascapes. His son Antoine Charles Horace Vernet, better known as Carle (1758–1836), also achieved success, especially for his equestrian scenes, but he abandoned his career in art following the execution of his sister via guillotine. His grandson Émile Jean-Horace Vernet (1789–1863), known as Horace, also went on to attain success in the medium and was best known for his battle scenes, as well as for the speed of his work. In the Sherlock Holmes story "The Adventure of the Greek Interpreter," Arthur Conan Doyle has Holmes claim that he is related to Vernet: "My ancestors were country squires, who appear to have led much the same life as is natural to their class. But, none the less, my turn that way is in my veins, and may have come with my grandmother, who was the sister of Vernet, the French artist." Doyle never specifies to which of the three Vernets Holmes was supposedly related but

given the detective's birth year of 1854 ("The Last Bow"), it would presumably have been Horace.

Henri-Joseph Harpignies (1819–1916) was a French landscape painter closely associated with the Barbizon school, an early realist movement. He became close friends with Corot.

Jean-Auguste-Dominique Ingres (1780–1867) was a prolific French Neoclassical painter whose works remained both scandalous and influential long after his death. He is considered an important precursor not only to early modernists such as Picasso and Matisse, but to later movements as well, especially expressionism and abstract expressionism.

Henri Fantin-Latour (1836–1904) was a French painter and lithographer, best known for his paintings of flowers and of groups of Parisian artists and writers, and his lithographs inspired by Wagner's *Ring* cycle. Despite his close friendships with early modernists such as Whistler and Monet, his own work remained more traditional. Whistler, however, did help to create a modest vogue for Fantin-Latour's work in the UK, where he became more popular for a time than in his native country.

Gobelin was the name of an entire family of French dyers, probably originating in Reims. Sometime in the fifteenth century, their progenitor, Jehan Gobelin (d. 1476), developed a particularly brilliant scarlet dyestuff, upon which the family's reputation subsequently rested. Several generations later, members of the family had become wealthy enough to purchase titles of nobility and hold state office. By the end of the seventeenth century none of them remained associated with their original trade, although their family name became synonymous with "tapestry" in multiple tongues, including English, French, Polish, and Dutch. The Gobelins Manufactory remains in operation today, run by the state.

Sèvres is a French commune in the southwestern suburbs of Paris, famous for its fine porcelain. By the mid-eighteenth century, Sèvres porcelain had become the dominant type in Europe.

Moustiers faience is a variety of earthenware pottery glazed with tin and/or lead, similar to Italian Majolica or Dutch Delftware, but manufactured in France. Legend has it that an Italian monk from Faenza shared the secret of faience-making with Pierre Clérissy (born ca. 1652). Pierre and his brother Antoine founded the first faience works in Moustiers sometime around 1679.

6. Jean-Baptiste Pigalle (1714–1785) was a French sculptor. He is said to have been the mentor of Madeleine-Élisabeth Pigalle (1751–1827), a French painter and his distant relative, but his name is best known today for its association with a Parisian red-light district.

Pierre Paul Puget (1620–1694) was a French Baroque painter and sculptor. Two of his major works, *Perseus and Andromeda* and *Alexander and Diogenes*, can be seen in the Louvre.

Bertel Thorvaldsen (1770–1844) was a Danish sculptor. Although born in Copenhagen, he spent most of his life (1797–1838) in Italy. He became a national hero in Denmark upon his return, and his house was later converted into a museum to house his works. Thorvaldsen is buried in the courtyard of the museum.

7. The dromon was the primary warship type of the Byzantine navy between the fifth and twelfth centuries CE. From the Greek δρόμων (*dromōn*: "racer").

A duumvir was either of a pair of jointly appointed magistrates in ancient Rome (from Latin *duumviri*, "two men"). The duumviri were the highest judicial magistrates in the cities of Roman Italy and its provinces.

8. Probably Fowey, a Cornish port town once important in the China clay (kaolinite) trade, but not associated with any major stone quarries.

9. Just as the device itself seems to be Cobwell's own creation, the phrase in the original, *hélio-taquin*, appears to be unique not only to Ray but to this novel. Its function, however, to cast reflected sunlight into people's eyes, is obvious.

10. A cyprinoid fish, known as a *gardon* in French; in English an ide, loach, or roach. The Greeny, like the Peully and Ingersham itself, appears to be one of Ray's geographical fabrications.

11. Ray has a fondness for obscure and obsolete lighting devices. The *lampe à lentille d'eau* employs a water-filled lens with at least once convex side to magnify the light of an oil lamp or candle. Curiously, its construction is very similar to Cobwell's homemade "helio-teaser," which is described just a few pages earlier.

12. The oft-retold story of Pygmalion is first attested in *De Cypro*, Philostephanus's history of Cyprus, but the version that has inspired dozens of European works down the centuries derives from the tenth book of Ovid's *Metamorphoses*, where Pygmalion, a Cypriot sculptor-king, despite vowing to remain celibate falls in love with a female statue he carved from ivory, which the goddess Aphrodite eventually brings to life. The name Galatea/Galathea does not appear in these early versions and was apparently added much later.

IV   TEA WITH THE PUMKINS LADIES

1. Anne of Cleves (1515–1557), the fourth wife of Henry VIII. Their marriage remained unconsummated and was quickly annulled.

2. A heraldic bird, originally identified as an eagle. Medieval bestiaries portray the alerion (or avalerion) as a mythological bird of which only one pair ever lived at a given time.

3. Lansquenet is a banking game played with an Italian forty-card deck. Its name derives obscurely from the German *Landsknecht* ("servant of the land or country"), in reference to a type of field drum employed by German mercenaries of the fifteenth and sixteenth centuries.

4. In all French editions, Molly addresses Ruth here as "Miss Snugg," an obvious error, which I have corrected.

V THE TERROR ON THE MOOR

1. Carabosse is the name of the wicked fairy godmother in later versions of Sleeping Beauty. The name first appears in the 1890 Russian ballet *The Sleeping Beauty* (Спящая красавиц), which was choreographed by Marius Petipa (1818–1910), with music by Pyotr Ilyich Tchaikovsky (1840–1893), after which the name became standard for the character until the animated Disney film, in which she is renamed Maleficent.

VI MR. DOOVE TELLS SOME STORIES

1. Daniel Quilp is a primary antagonist in Charles Dickens's 1840 novel *The Old Curiosity Shop*. Dickens presents Quilp as mean of spirit and foul of temper, and of grotesque appearance: "so low in stature as to be quite a dwarf, though his head and face were large enough for a giant. His black eyes were restless, sly and cunning, his mouth and chin, bristly with the stubble of a coarse hard beard; and his complexion was one of that kind which never looks clean or wholesome." Quilp is Dickens's most monstrous character. Ray's description of Pycroft clearly borrows from the description of Quilp quoted above.

2. Joseph Justus Scaliger (1540–1609) was a French Calvinist scholar and critic who was best known for expanding the notion of classical history beyond the Greeks and the Romans to include the history of the Persians, Egyptians, Babylonians, and Hebrews. As a critic, he made many enemies, especially among the Jesuits.

3. Gerolamo Cardano (1501–1576) was an Italian mathematician, physicist, chemist, biologist, physician, astronomer, astrologer, philosopher, author,

and gambler. One of the most important mathematicians of the Renaissance, he played a key role in the foundation of probability studies and was the earliest to introduce binomial coefficients and the binomial theorem to the West. He authored over 200 scientific works. His 1557 *Actio prima in calumniatorem* (First action against the slanderer) was a reply to Scaliger.

4. Chemist, botanist, and politician François-Vincent Raspail (1794–1878) created *Raspail*, a brand of dessert liqueur with a hygienic aim, in 1847.

5. The Engadine, or Engadin, is a long, high-walled valley region in the eastern Swiss Alps that follows the route of the River Inn.

6. Turnhout is a Belgian city in the Flemish province of Antwerp. Nietdeug ("No Good") was an archetypal Dutch troublemaker figure who somewhat resembled Krazy Kat, Sluggo from *Nancy*, or Dennis the Menace. He appeared in several of the Épinal prints, such as *De Lotgevallen von Nietdeug* (*The Misadventures of No Good*). The story of the sugarloaf involves a negligent delivery boy assigned to deliver a sugarloaf (a conical construction similar in size and shape to a large mortar shell). All these images are excellent examples of why Épinal prints are often considered to be important precursors to modern comics.

7. *Le Distrait* ("The Distracted Man") is based on Ménalque, a man of variable mind, one of the character types described in the canonical 1688 work *Caractères* by the French moralist Jean de La Bruyère (1645–1696).

8. Gerrit Dou (1613–1675) was a painter of the Dutch Golden Age. Rembrandt was his mentor.

9. The American homeopath Hawley Harvey Crippen (1862–1910) was executed at Pentonville Prison for the murder of his wife Cora Henrietta Crippen. A human torso found buried beneath the brick floor of the Crippen's cellar was identified as Cora's, despite the fact that the head and limbs were never found. The case is also significant as the first in which Marconi's wireless radio played a role in the arrest. The events of Crippen's case provided the inspiration for Arthur Machen's 1927 short story "The Islington Mystery."

VII THE PASSION OF REVINUS

1. Ray almost certainly refers here to *Storm Off a Sea Coast* (also known as *The Breakwater* or *The Storm*) by Jacob van Ruisdael (1629–1682), but it is to be noted that his uncle Salomon van Ruysdael (ca. 1602–1670) painted similar,

though generally less tempestuous, scenes. Jacob van Ruisdael painted multiple images of storms at sea, but the aforementioned work, today in the collection of the Louvre, is considered a masterpiece and is by far the most famous.

2. The Paragon Umbrella frame, patented by Samuel Fox in 1852, featured a U-section of string steel that was far superior to any competitor at the time. To satisfy the increasing demand, Fox established an umbrella works at Amiens, France, in 1860.

VIII INTO THE PENTAGRAM

1. The Italian playwright, poet, and satirist Pietro Aretino (1492–1556) is particularly well-remembered for his *Sonetti Lussuriosi* (*Lustful Sonnets*), which he wrote as accompaniments for *I Modi* (*The Ways*, or *The Sixteen Pleasures*), a book of exquisite and explicitly pornographic engravings by Marcantonio Raimondi (ca. 1470/1482–ca. 1534) based on an earlier set of paintings by Giulio Romano (1499–1546). Although Aretino had successfully weathered many controversies already, the outrage that this little book generated forced him to flee Rome temporarily (Raimondi was imprisoned, though Aretino later won his release).

Most English translations of his work are recent, so Ray's repeated suggestion that Doove was translating his sonnets is a heavily loaded allusion. During a 2008 performance at Cadogan Hall of composer Michael Nyman's *8 Lust Songs*, which was set to half of Aretino's sequence, the organizers were forced to withdraw the printed programs based on accusations of obscenity. The US CD release of the composition remains one of the few classical music releases ever to bear a "Parental Advisory Explicit Content" label. Triggs merely blushes.

2. The "pear of anguish," a.k.a. "choke pear," was a torture device, possibly apocryphal.

IX THE 28 DAYS OF MR. BASKET

1. The Viennese physician Josef Breuer (1842–1925) was Sigmund Freud's mentor. His work in the 1880s with patient Bertha Pappenheim (a.k.a. Anna O) led to the development of the "talking cure" (the cathartic method), and created the necessary foundation for psychoanalysis. However, unlike Freud, he did not consider

sexual issues to be the exclusive cause of neurotic symptoms, so Basket's application of psychoanalysis here is that of Breuer rather than Freud.

2. Wackford Squeers is the corrupt and abusive schoolmaster of Dotheboys Hall in Charles Dickens's novel *Nicholas Nickleby, or The Life and Adventures of Nicholas Nickleby, Containing a Faithful Account of the Fortunes, Misfortunes, Uprisings, Downfallings, and Complete Career of the Nickleby Family*, which was published serially from 1838 to 1839. Dickens claimed that the character of Squeers was a composite of several schoolmasters he encountered while investigating abuses in the boys' schools of Yorkshire, but evidence suggests the primary model was one William Shaw, who ran William Shaw's Academy in Bowes. Shaw was taken to court after a boy was blinded at his school. In the novel, Squeers is ultimately sent to Australia.

3. A fenestra is a small oval or round window. The term usually has an anatomical meaning, referring to openings in bone, but Jean Ray employs it here in its literal sense.

A SOMBER AND SOLITARY GENTLEMAN

1. Oliver Cromwell (1599–1658), mentioned several times earlier in the text, who served as Lord Protector from 1653 until his death in 1658.

Archaeologist, caver, father, educator, podcaster, activist, translator, DJ, World Fantasy Award–winner, Scott Nicolay has been many things. But never a minister.

THE SCHOOL OF THE STRANGE

1. *Spells*, Michel de Ghelderode

2. *Whiskey Tales*, Jean Ray

3. *Cruise of Shadows: Haunted Stories of Land and Sea*, Jean Ray

4. *Waystations of the Deep Night*, Marcel Brion

5. *The Great Nocturnal: Tales of Dread*, Jean Ray

6. *Circles of Dread*, Jean Ray

7. *Malpertuis*, Jean Ray

8. *The Impersonal Adventure*, Marcel Béalu

9. *The City of Unspeakable Fear*, Jean Ray